Unavoidable

ISBN: 978-1-951122-18-8 (paperback)
ISBN: 978-1-951122-23-2 (ebook)
LCCN: 2020949480
Copyright © 2021 by Geoff Habiger & Coy Kissee
Cover Art: © Ian Bristow
Cover Design: Ian Bristow

Printed in the United States of America.

Shadow Dragon Press
9 Mockingbird Hill Rd
Tijeras, New Mexico 87059
www.shadowdragonpress.com
info@shadowdragonpress.com

Other Books Available from Geoff and Coy

Saul Imbierowicz Series
Unremarkable
Untouchable

Constable Inspector Lunaria Adventures
Wrath of the Fury Blade
Joy of the Widow's Tears

UNAVOIDABLE

By

Geoff Habiger
and
Coy Kissee

"I don't need to tell you that, what determines a man's legacy is often what isn't seen."

~ J. Edgar Hoover

Chapter 1

"I'm telling you, they got lucky."

"Lucky? No way!" Christian said, emphatically. "The A's dominated the Cubs in the World Series. Chicago didn't even show up."

I turned to look out of the car's window. Christian was right; the Cubs hadn't been able to handle the A's pitching. All of Chicago had cheered when we'd won the pennant, and then we'd all drowned our sorrows in illegal whiskey and beer when the A's nearly swept us in the World Series. I turned back to look at Christian. "If Hornsby—"

"Look, Saul," Christian said, interrupting me. "You're going to beat yourself up more and more if you keep playing 'what ifs' in your head. Get over it. The series ended five months ago. You're not going to do yourself any favors with the season starting in a couple of weeks. Besides," he gave me a quick glance, "I told you not to make such large bets with Stutzman and Friel."

"It's not about the money," I said, although losing a sawbuck to each of the two agents on Ness's team, both from Pennsylvania and both rabid fans of the Philadelphia Athletics, had stung. "It's the way that they rubbed it in, especially Friel."

Christian chuckled. "You know, for a vampire, you sure have a thin skin when it comes to baseball.

Especially the Cubs."

"I do not."

"So, Game 3 wasn't 'the greatest debacle, the most terrific flop in the history of the World Series' according to Mr. Ed Burns of the Tribune?"

"Hey, don't you start. Everybody knows that Hack Wilson lost the ball in the sun. It wasn't his fault."

"Thin. Skin." Christian taunted me again. "Well, you'd better get used to it. I think Philadelphia is going to make it to the series again this year."

"We'll beat them this time."

Christian gave a noncommittal shrug. "Maybe. The Cards look pretty good."

"No way will the Cardinals win the pennant."

"Care to put some money on that?" Christian gave me a mischievous smile, and I couldn't help but laugh.

"I think I'll pass. I've learned my lesson." I went back to looking out of the car's window at the bulk of the Eastern State Penitentiary. This is where Al Capone had been put away after his arrest for carrying a concealed weapon last year. It was a massive, imposing building, and it reminded me of castles that I'd seen in books. I checked my watch for the dozenth time since we'd arrived. "Come on. When's this show going to get started?"

Christian glanced at his own watch. "There's still time. The warden said that they weren't going to release Capone until after ten. We're lucky that we're even here."

I grunted an acknowledgement. "Whose ass did Ness have to kiss to get the news?"

"I think it was a professional courtesy. Since the warden is secretly releasing Capone a day before the 'official' date, I'm sure that he wanted us to know about it."

"Maybe," I offered. "Too bad we won't be able to see the expressions on the faces of all of those people and reporters who are going to show up tomorrow for nothing."

"Oh, I'm sure that somebody will snap a few photos of the event. That way they can howl about being duped by the warden in the papers."

I smiled at the image, and then turned my thoughts back to Capone. "Still, it's not like this has been a real hardship for Capone."

"He's spent nearly a year in prison," Christian stated. "Capone's always lived a lavish lifestyle, so prison life had to have been hard."

"It's been barely ten months," I said. "And have you seen the photos of his cell? It had a nice rug and a bed with a warm, thick blanket. Plus, he had a desk, and an armchair, and *two* lamps."

"Don't forget the radio," Christian added.

"Tell me again how Capone was being punished? His cell was almost as nice as his place at the Lexington."

"It was still a cell."

My only response to that was another grunt. "He was on vacation," I said. I turned to look at Christian. "And I think he's been involved with those recent attacks in Chicago."

"You mean the diner?"

I nodded. "That, and the gunfight at that speakeasy a month back."

Christian shook his head. "As far as we know, those attacks weren't related to anybody that Capone has a grudge against, and they didn't seem to be a grab for power or territory by his organization. Besides, how'd he order a hit from inside the pen?"

I turned in my seat and stared, open-mouthed, at Christian. After a moment, he acknowledged the obvious. "Okay, okay. Capone the gangster and Capone the vampire could have easily done it. But I still don't think that he had anything to do with those attacks."

"You don't think that Capone would stoop to killing innocent children?" I asked, anger and sadness fighting each other as to which of my emotions would be the one to bubble to the surface first. "A little girl was killed at the diner. A survivor said that she was holding the case that had the bomb in it when it went off."

"Capone is a monster—in both the figurative and the literal sense." I ignored the veiled barb in that comment. "But the diner was up on the North Side, in a part of the city that normally isn't under Capone's influence. If anybody was making a play, it was Bugs Moran."

I shrugged to acknowledge his point. "But Moran has been pretty quiet lately. I don't think it was him. Plus, a bombing isn't his style."

"Gangsters have styles?"

"You know what I mean," I said. "But it is strange that there haven't been any direct attacks on Capone's organization. I mean, while he's been 'on hiatus' here." I gestured to the massive structure outside. "We haven't heard a peep from Mr. Brown or his master since Capone was arrested. Why didn't they make a move to try to take over Capone's territory? Last May, it felt like we were on the verge of a full-scale vampire gang war, but then as soon as Capone gets pinched, nothing happens."

"Maybe Mr. Brown's master got what she wanted?"

"I don't think so. Something else had to have happened."

"What, though? We've not seen Mr. Brown since he fled the pier in Atlantic City," Christian said.

I gave yet another shrug. Christian and I had beaten this topic to death since our return from New Jersey. We were no closer to figuring out what was going on now than we were a year ago. Mr. Brown had apparently disappeared from the face of the Earth.

"When we get back to Chicago, we should practice your 'Renfield' routine," I said, changing the topic. "With Capone back in town, it may come in handy."

"Don't call it that," Christian growled while he unconsciously fingered the silver cross that he wore around his neck. "You know that I hate being referred to by that name."

"No, you hate that I have any power over you because of our connection."

"That, too."

"Capone used the word procurator. I could call you that instead of Renfield."

Christian turned to me in a huff. "Just call me your partner. That's what I am, despite this abominable curse you've afflicted me with."

Still winning friends, Sarah's voice taunted me. *You know he's going to sit and fume for the rest of the day now.*

Oh, shut up, I told her.

Fine, be a putz *and don't apologize. I was getting tired of all of your yammering anyway.*

You should listen to your sister, my mother felt compelled to add. *You know your partner doesn't like it when you call him that name.*

And what should I call him, then?

Are you meshuga? My father suddenly asked. *You call him your partner, because that's what he is. I didn't get to be supervisor at the plant—*

"I'm sorry," I said quickly, cutting off my father's voice. I'd heard enough about his job to last me a lifetime—which might be forever now. "I know that you don't like me to use that name."

I waited, but Christian continued sulking. I bit back my frustration. "I won't use it again... partner." I raised my eyes to see that Christian had relaxed, somewhat.

"You're more than that, too," I said. "You're a really good friend."

Christian angrily held up his index finger. "I'm your partner, you unholy abomination, but I am *not* your friend."

I put my hand to my heart. "You always say the nicest things." I gave a little laugh to let him know that his bluster didn't bother me. At least, I assumed it was bluster. He called me an abomination against God so frequently that it felt like how my mom always referred to Dad as a lazy schmuck when he did something that she didn't like.

"Whatever you want to call it, we have a... bond now. We need to practice using it so that we can deal with Capone when he gets back to Chicago."

Christian pointed to the rear gate of the penitentiary, which was swinging open. "Speak of the devil."

"I'm sitting right here," I deadpanned. Christian sighed, rolled his eyes, and shook his head as he started the car. A single Dodge sedan pulled out of the gate and passed us. I could make out Al Capone sitting in the back seat. Christian put our beat-up Buick Standard Six into gear, and we followed Capone's car.

Chapter 2

"Don't lose him," I said, as Capone's car turned west to head out of Philadelphia.

"His is the only other car on the road," Christian said, gesturing to the empty road with one hand. "Besides, we know where he's going."

"If the warden's information was right."

"It was. Why would he lie to Ness?"

"And if Capone sticks to the plan," I added. Christian didn't have a reply for that, and I felt a small tingle of victory.

We were approaching an intersection. Capone's car slowed, and then went on straight up the road. I said, "Uh. Weren't they supposed to turn if they were going to the train station? Like they were supposed to?"

Christian's reply was to gun the engine. We sped through the intersection. He pointed to a sign that read "Airport 5 miles".

"That's where they're going. He's going to fly home," Christian said, sounding smug.

"Great," I said. "I've never been on a plane before." Christian started to say something, but I laughed to let him know that I was joking.

The road curved to the left, and Capone's sedan disappeared around the bend, briefly hidden by a cluster of trees and shrubs. As we made the turn, a Model A

Ford raced up along a side road, the car spraying dirt and gravel over us as it skidded onto the highway.

"Mother of God!" Christian swore, and jerked the wheel. We avoided colliding with their bumper by mere inches, and my dead heart raced as I had a vision of being decapitated in a horrible car crash on a Pennsylvanian county road.

That would be a great headline, quipped Sarah. *"Mighty Vampire Slain in Car Crash."*

I ignored my sister's sarcasm as Christian kept us on the road. "Crazy country drivers," he complained.

Something wasn't right about this, and my arm hairs stood up. I looked over at the Ford and then I spotted it. "The plates," I said, pointing. "They're from Illinois."

Just then, the Ford accelerated. A window on the passenger side rolled down, and I saw the distinctive shape of a Tommy Gun poke out of the car.

"Gun!" I yelled, just as the staccato of bullets ripped through the air. Christian jerked the wheel, but it was suddenly clear that they were shooting at Capone. Bullets impacted with a loud THWANG, THWANG, THWANG on the rear of the Dodge. The big car struggled to accelerate and started to swerve, the driver trying to break the gunner's aim.

I felt our car slow a bit, and I turned to Christian. "What are you doing?"

"Staying alive."

"And what happens if Al Capone is gunned down outside of jail a day *before* he's supposed to be released? I'm not thrilled about saving Capone's life, but we can't let him be killed like this. The press will have a field day, and Ness will never let us hear the end of it."

Christian hesitated, and I could hear him grinding

his teeth. Then he said, "Blessed Jesus, please protect us." Our car accelerated, and I pulled out my gun and rolled down my window.

Ooh... think you can actually hit something this time? Sarah taunted me.

Shut up! I know what I'm doing.

Sure, nudnick. *I'm still surprised that Ness even lets you have a gun.*

Well, I can't go all fangy when we're dealing with regular goons.

Fangy?

It's a word, I told her, as I pointed the gun at the Ford.

"Your safety is still on!" Christian yelled.

I felt the heat rising on my face as I thumbed the safety off and tried to ignore the peals of laughter coming from Sarah.

Christian pulled along the driver's side of the Model A. The RAT-A-TAT-TAT explosion of bullets continued from the other side of the car as a tongue of flame licked out of the Tommy Gun's barrel with each bullet. The bullets continued to strike the rear of Capone's car, sparks flying with each impact.

The driver of the Model A finally noticed us. I could see his eyes go wide. I don't know if he thought that we were the cops or if he thought that we were some of Capone's men, but I saw him take one hand off the wheel and reach into his coat.

"Not today, buddy." I aimed at the car's front wheel, like Barney Cloonan had said to do if you wanted to disable a vehicle. We needed these guys alive in order to see who had sent them after Capone. Was this just a normal gang thing—some of Moran's men, or another gang—looking to make a statement? Or was this the first shots in a large-scale vampire gang war? Either way, taking out the head of your rivals was a tried and true method that Capone himself had used more than a few times. But how did they know that Capone would be let out a day early?

I shook the thoughts away and concentrated on my aim. Our car and the Ford were both weaving all over the road, nearly colliding with each other a few times. I pulled the trigger.

The gun bucked in my hand, and I continued to pull the trigger. In a short time, the last casing was ejected, and the slide locked back. There were four neat holes in the Ford's fender, but the tire was still in one piece.

Nice shooting there, Wild Bill, Sarah taunted. *It's truly amazing that you even hit the car. Maybe if it was the size of a barn you might have better luck.*

I didn't have time to argue with her. The driver of the Ford raised his weapon, a small revolver. He didn't bother to roll down his window, and just fired. Glass exploded, and Christian swerved. Two bullets struck my door, two hit the hood, and one hit the windscreen, which erupted in a spider web of cracks, but didn't shatter.

"Don't worry," said Christian. "It's bulletproof."

Just then, the final bullet from the other driver struck the windscreen. More cracks appeared, followed by a small hole.

"Well, it's *supposed* to be bulletproof."

"Damnit, I'm going to do this the easy way." I felt my fangs extend inside my mouth.

So, now it's okay to get all 'fangy'? Sarah asked, her tone mocking. *What are you going to do, bite their car?*

"Get me alongside them!" I yelled to Christian.

Christian applied more throttle, and we pulled alongside the Ford. I opened my door and stepped onto the running board, the grey pavement racing by inches under my feet. I didn't think. I didn't pause. I just acted.

I jumped off of the running board and landed on the rear of the Ford, my fingers digging into the metal frame like it was soft dough. Through the rear window, I could see the gunner pulling in his weapon and turning to face me. I leaped forward just as he pulled the trigger. Several bullets exploded out of the car where I had just been. He stared at me, his mouth wide in shock, while the driver was trying to keep the car on the road.

I reached through the shattered window and grabbed the steering wheel. We needed to get off the road, to keep them from killing Capone. Or me. With a quick jerk, I ripped the steering wheel from the driver's hands and turned it, hard. The car turned sharply and then shuddered, the rear wheels skipping once before we were suddenly airborne.

Oh shit! What the hell did I do?

I jumped clear as the Ford tumbled, rolling along the highway, glass shattering and covering the road in a sparkling carpet. The car finally came to rest on its wheels, but it wouldn't be able to drive any further.

I landed hard, hitting my knee, and rolled as well, but I fared better than the Ford. As I stood up, my knee almost gave out, but I was already starting to heal. Past the ruined Ford, I could see Capone's Dodge continue to scream down the road.

"Figures."

Behind me, Christian slowed to a stop. He opened the door and stood on the running board. "Are they all right?"

A year ago, I would have thrown him an angry reply at a comment like that; it seemed that he cared more about the goons than me. But we'd been working together long enough now that I knew that he knew that I healed easily from these kinds of scrapes. Besides, we needed these two *schmos* alive if we wanted to learn why they'd attacked Capone.

I dusted broken glass and road grit off my coat. The Ford was a crumpled mass, looking like a tin can that had been used too long in a game of kick the can. "I hope so," I said, as I walked over to the wreck.

I could smell the gasoline leaking from the ruptured tank. Mixed with it was the sweet scent of blood. I heard Christian close his door, followed by the crunch of his shoes on the broken glass.

The driver's side was smashed so badly that I had to lean down in order to see into the car. The inside was a mess, as were the two men. Amazingly, the passenger was still clutching the Tommy Gun, but he also had part of the door frame sticking through his neck.

Ooh... look at the carnage, Saul, cooed Moira's voice in my head. I could picture her licking her lips in a seductive gesture. *I didn't know you had it in you.*

I shook the thought of her away and turned my attention to the driver. I could hear the faint beating of his heart. "This one is still alive," I said, as Christian circled the wreck. "But his partner won't be walking out of here."

Christian leaned down, and I saw him go pale as he looked into the car. "You okay?" I asked. Christian swallowed, closed his eyes for a moment, crossed himself, and then nodded.

A soft groan came from the driver, and I pulled hard

on the door. The metal creaked and popped at first, and then, with a loud squeal, the door ripped open. I knelt down and gently smacked the man's cheeks.

"Wake up, buddy. You alright?" His eyelids fluttered and slowly opened.

"Wha..."

"You were in a car wreck. Help's on the way," I lied. I could tell that his injuries were too severe. Any help that might be coming would arrive too late. I needed to act fast to find out what we needed to know.

"Just relax," I commanded. "Tell me why you were shooting at Al Capone."

The combination of the trauma of the accident and my gift of persuasion seemed to have the desired effect.

"Want... wanted to s... send a mess—age to Capone." He licked his lips, and I was suddenly reminded of a February night a year ago when I was lying in a hospital bed after having been shot by Capone.

"What message?" I asked.

"That he... he's not un... untouchable. We weren't to k—kill him... just show him he could be re... reached." The man's head rolled to look at me. "That we know his... secrets." He gave a small smile at the remark.

"Who wanted to send the message?" I asked.

"M... man in..." he coughed, blood spurting from his lips and hitting me in the face. I had to force myself to keep from licking it up.

"What man? Who told you to scare Capone?"

"Never g—gave his name," the driver looked up into my face. "Pale... man, dressed in... b—brown." He lifted his left hand and poked it at me. "Are you... a Fed?"

I was surprised by the question, but I nodded. The man gave another smile, or maybe it was supposed to

13

be a smirk. "The man... he said that if... if we ran into t—two Feds... to tell them that he ha-hasn't for... gotten w—what they did in—" he coughed out more blood, "in Atlantic City."

I looked up to Christian, who was leaning in the passenger side window. I wasn't sure if his eyes were wider than mine.

More coughs came from the driver. "Where did you meet this man in brown? Where is he?"

"He... h—" his voice fell silent and his head dropped to his chest. I heard the final beat of his heart.

"Damnit!" I struck the side of the car hard enough that it rocked. "We were *this* close to learning where Mr. Brown is."

Christian was ignoring me. He was pulling open the gunner's coat, rifling through his pockets.

"We haven't heard a peep from Brown or his master since Atlantic City, and then this comes out of nowhere." I gestured to the ruined car. "And now our one lead to find Brown has died."

Yeah, great job nudnik, Sarah taunted in my head. *Maybe next time, don't be too 'fangy'.*

I don't need you telling me I screwed up.

Sure you do. How else are you going to learn? That's what sisters are for.

"Finally," Christian muttered. I looked over and saw him examining something in his hands. He glanced at me, with a slight smile on his face. He tossed something to me, and I caught it. A black matchbook. I flipped it over, and printed in bright, blood-red ink was the name "Pandora's Legacy – Pool Hall" and a Chicago address.

"Kind of a strange name for a pool hall," Christian said.

Chapter 3

Christian handed me a newspaper as we entered the Federal Building in Chicago. "I told you someone would get a picture," he said.

It was a small photo below the fold, but it showed the faces of a shocked crowd who had gathered outside the penitentiary in Pennsylvania hoping to see the famous gangster. I smiled. "Serves them right for fawning over a man like Capone."

"Monster, not man," Christian corrected, as we entered the elevator. I acknowledged his opinion with a grunt.

We got off on our floor and walked to the office. Things had gotten better lately, as most of the team that worked with Ness had started accepting me. I still got harassed for being a rookie, but even Friel had started treating me better—at least after he'd won that money off me after the World Series.

Paul Robsky and Cloonan greeted us as we entered the office. "Hey, Stan," Cloonan called to me, using the alias that Ness had given me. "How was babysitting a gangster?"

"Maybe you can get back to doing some real police work, Kowalski," added Robsky.

"Breeze off, Paul," I said, "At least we know what a real gangster looks like."

The way Paul laughed let me know that he'd taken my ribbing in stride. That hadn't always been the case, but, like I said, they were treating me better. None of them knew my real name, or that I was really a vampire, and I was fine with that. The fewer people that knew about what I was, the better.

Christian and I hung up our coats and hats and walked over to Eliot Ness's office at the back of the room. We had driven all night after the encounter with the goons who had been gunning for Capone, and Christian looked like he could use some sleep. I could have done with a pit stop at my apartment to drink some blood, but we needed to let our boss know what had happened. Christian gave a knock and Ness told us to enter.

"How was your trip?" Ness asked. "I heard that Capone had quite the welcome back party at Little Florence last night."

"He must have been looking to celebrate his escape from death as well as from prison," I said as I closed the door.

"Death?" Ness leaned back in his chair, the single word both a question and an order to tell him what happened.

"Someone set up an ambush for Capone," said Christian. On our drive back to Chicago, we'd decided to keep Mr. Brown's role in this to ourselves—at least until it was the right time to share it—and agreed that it would be best if Ness heard it from Christian.

"Two goons were waiting in a car and gave chase," I said. "They shot up Capone's car, turning it into Swiss cheese."

"They weren't the best shots either," added Christian, "as they never got close to hitting Capone."

"Sending a message," Ness said, nodding his head. Eliot Ness was no fool.

"That's what we think," Christian said. "These people knew that," he held up one finger, "he was getting out a day early," he held up a second finger, "and that he was going to fly home. That means that they had inside information."

Ness sat forward and placed his arms on his desk. "So, who's sending a message to Capone?"

"Mr. Brown," I said, forgetting our agreement and blurting out the name. Ness gave an aggravated sigh, and I caught a glimpse of Christian's frown out of the corner of my eye.

No wonder your partner hates you, taunted Sarah.

You never could follow simple directions, added Dad.

"It's the truth," I added quickly, turning to look to Christian for confirmation. "Right, partner?"

Christian nodded. "One of the men said that he'd been hired by Mr. Brown to send a message to Capone."

"And you have this guy in custody so we can confirm this?" Ness asked.

"No," Christian said, looking down at the floor. "He died from his injuries at the scene."

"Of course he did." Ness threw an accusing look at me.

"Hey! It's not my fault," I said. "I didn't know the car was going to roll like that."

"You practically pulled the steering wheel off," said Christian. "What did you think would happen?"

I stared at him, wide-eyed. He hadn't been upset about it on our drive home, but now he was ratting me out. I could feel a tightening in my gut.

Did you think that, just maybe, your partner is trying to help you out? Dad asked. *Of course not! Why am I not surprised? He's only blaming you because you don't know* bupkis *about cars.*

Dad was right. I forced myself to not bite back and said, "I just wanted to turn them off the road. To get Capone out of their aim." I looked at Ness, trying to appear apologetic. "I didn't know that the car would roll like it did."

Turning back to Christian I added, "Maybe if I got to drive sometimes, I'd have known that would happen." *Yeah, I had to get at least one jab in.*

"Mary, Mother of God, no! I'm still paying for the transmission that I had to get repaired after the one," he held up a finger, "*one* time that I let you drive. Never again."

Despite Christian's anger—

Well-deserved anger, corrected Sarah.

I could feel the tension in the room ease.

And maybe that was your partner's plan all along, Dad said.

"We're sure that Mr. Brown is involved," Christian said to Ness. "The driver was badly hurt and had no reason to lie to us. Plus, Saul used his... *influence* on the driver."

Ness considered what Christian had said, looking up at the ceiling for a moment. "So, why now? Why'd they wait to make a move on Capone? Why just scare him? Hell, everybody in the whole world knew that Capone was in that prison for the past ten months. If your kind," he waved a hand toward me, "are so powerful, why didn't they attack Capone in prison?"

"We don't know," I said, looking down at my shoes.

Christian and I had discussed this at length as well on our drive back. We hadn't been able to come up with anything.

"You tried to tell me there was a vampire gang war starting up last year." Ness was speaking casually, but there was also disappointment as bitter as day-old coffee. "Yet these other vampires didn't do a single thing while Capone was in prison. Do you want to know *why* they didn't do anything?"

Christian and I stood there dumbly. I could tell that Ness wasn't expecting us to answer.

"Because these other vampires *don't exist.*"

I apparently failed at keeping my expression neutral, because Ness smirked at me.

"If there was another vampire gang, they'd have done something to get rid of the king vampire while he was locked away."

"But what about Mr. Brown?" I asked. "He tried to kill you. Are you saying he doesn't exist?"

Ness waved my words away. "What about him? We've not seen or heard from him since Atlantic City. Maybe he died there, and we didn't know it."

I could feel my hands starting to shake. *No way did Mr. Brown die in Atlantic City.* Sure, we beat him up pretty good while saving Ness, but I was sure that he didn't die.

"The driver said it was a man in all brown clothes who paid them to attack Capone," Christian said. "Even if it wasn't the same Mr. Brown, we should still investigate this event. There may be more attacks, more violence. At least let Saul and I look into who ordered the attack."

"No." Ness didn't even pause to consider the option. Before Christian or I could say anything, Ness said, "I don't want to waste our resources going after two-bit, wannabe gangsters who are just looking to give Capone a fright. No, the best way to get Capone is on his taxes."

Ness must have seen me rolling my eyes, because he pointed at me as he said, "We've been having luck getting a couple of gangsters put away on this tax thing. If we can show that Capone earns an income from his various activities, then we can put him away for tax evasion. That's how we'll stop Capone."

I was going to say something, to disagree with Ness—yeah, I'm a bit stupid that way—but even my supernatural speed wasn't fast enough to beat Christian.

"Capone is a monster," he said, vehemently. "He's an abomination before God, and a murderer and criminal, and you want to try and take him down for not paying his taxes? We need to stop playing around and take the fight to Capone. Now that he's out of prison, he'll be starting up where he left off. Nobody is safe around a monster like that—"

I wondered what that meant for me.

"—and he needs to be destroyed. The only way that Chicago will be safe is when he has a stake in his heart."

Ness and I both stared at Christian, wondering if he was finished.

How do you let this creature serve as your procurator? Came Moira's sultry purr. *You should finish him off before he decides to put a stake in* your *heart.*

Ness was the first to recover his voice. "I will not condone the murder of a man—"

"Monster," Christian spat.

"A citizen of this city, even if he is a gangster."

Christian glared at Ness.

"Or a monster. Capone's death will not fix the problem, nor will it serve our purpose."

This time, I beat Christian to the punch. "And what purpose is that?"

"To show these criminals that no man—or monster," Ness nodded to Christian, "is above the law. Tax evasion may not give the satisfaction that a trial for murder or racketeering may have, but it still has teeth." Ness gave a smile and looked at me.

"So, what do you want us to do?" I asked.

Ness picked up a pencil from his desk and leaned back in his chair. "The aim of our case against Capone must change. We need to know about his finances— how he gets paid. While he's still the target of my investigation, he is no longer the main focus. I'm pulling you two off of watching Capone."

"What?" Christian and I said at the same time.

"So, we're letting the monster out of our sight," Christian said.

"You know," Ness said, "I expected that to come from him." He pointed the pencil at me.

Christian gave a shrug that was far from being apologetic. I'd seen the same look last year when Christian had suggested that we go to Atlantic City. Ness must have recognized it as well.

"Don't you get any ideas. I will not stand for any insubordination this time. If you want to stay on my team, you will stay the hell away from Capone. You will do what I tell you to do, or you'll be looking for new jobs."

Christian and I looked at each other. I don't know if it was due to our being partners, or if our special connection was working, but we reached an unspoken agreement.

"We understand," I said. "What do you want us to

do?" There was a decided lack of enthusiasm in my voice, but Ness either didn't notice or didn't care.

"There's a speakeasy over on the Lower West Side that we think is linked to Capone. I need you to watch the place and see if anybody of importance goes there. Don't go inside. Don't confront anybody. Just record the time when anybody of importance goes there."

"How will we know who's important?" I asked.

"If we have a picture of them in our books, they're important."

I nodded, already dreading this new assignment. It was far from being exciting or glamorous. It was also far from Capone, which, I suppose, was Ness's point.

"We'd better brush up on the mug shots, then," Christian said, turning to open the door.

"Oh boy, I can't wait," I said. Ness ignored my sarcasm and went back to his own work.

Chapter 4

"Why did we agree to do this?" I asked, staring out the car window as a light rain fell. Christian had not had time to repair the glass from our encounter in Pennsylvania, and a spider web of cracks filled the windscreen. We'd been watching the speakeasy for only a few hours, and the rain meant that almost nobody had shown up. Those that had were nearly impossible to identify due to the weather.

"Because I like my job," Christian said. He was quietly drumming his fingers on the steering wheel.

"You like being bored out of your mind?"

"I like having a steady income. And, in case you forgot, there was a big crash in the stock market last year. A lot of folks have lost their jobs."

I waved my hand to the rain-soaked street. "This isn't a job. We've been sent to sit in the corner. We're being punished because Ness and his kind don't have the balls to confront Capone."

"You'd prefer a gunfight with Capone on Michigan Avenue?"

You lost the last one of those, Sarah commented.

"No. But you know this tax stuff is *dreck*. Capone will beat any case we can bring against him. He owns all of the judges."

"So how would bringing him up on murder or racketeering charges be any different?" Christian sounded exasperated, and I realized that we'd had this conversation many times before, and we never got anywhere.

The L rattled by overhead, and I rubbed my chin. My mind turned to the news story I'd read in the morning paper. "Did you hear about what happened at Grove Undertakers last night?"

Christian shook his head and continued to stare out of the window.

"Somebody broke in and stole a corpse."

This caused Christian to turn and look at me. "Who would steal a corpse?"

I shrugged. "The paper also said that a night guard was killed, though they didn't find his body. All they found was a lot of blood."

Christian shook his head, but seemed uninterested, so I told him the most interesting item from the story. "The corpse that was stolen was one of the victims from the diner bombing."

This caused Christian to stare at me, his mouth forming an "O" of surprise.

"Maybe it wasn't a corpse at all," I mused. "What if the bomb victim had been a vampire, and it took him a while to heal up after the blast?"

"We don't know that. There could be another explanation."

"Do you really believe that?" I asked. "A vampire makes the most sense. The evidence is practically shouting the fact."

"Now you're just jumping to conclusions. There are other possible reasons." He paused, staring at the rain for a moment, and then said, "What does this have to do with anything?"

"That the vampire war is still brewing. They're just using different tactics. They're trying to keep the violence out of the news. They don't want to attract any attention."

Christian gave a snort. "From whom?"

"From us. The Night Watchers."

Christian held up a finger. "One, you are not a member of the Night Watchers. And two," he put up another finger, "Why should they care? You and I are not a threat to anybody. Mr. Brown and his master know that we can't stop Capone, and we couldn't stop Brown, either. Why would they care what we did? They have no reason to keep this quiet."

"But now we have a lead that we didn't have before," I continued. "We know that Brown is still out there and is still a threat. We need to find the proof."

Christian reached into his coat and pulled out the matchbook. The red lettering stood out sharply on the black cover. He turned it over in his hands a few times.

"There's a clue at that pool hall," I said. "About Mr. Brown and what they are going to try against Capone. You know that a vampire war is still possible. Sure, we don't know why they didn't do anything when he was in prison, but now that Capone is out, there's more of a chance that it will happen. We should be following up on *this*," I pointed to the matchbook. "Not staring at a dive, and hoping that some important goon shows up."

Christian closed his eyes. "These monsters won't care who gets in their way when they start to fight. Ness means well, but he doesn't know what they are capable of. He sees Capone as a gangster first, and a vampire second. He doesn't see the threat for what it is."

"So, let's ditch this assignment and go check out the

pool hall."

"We can do both," Christian hedged. "With my... abilities as your partner, I can detect any vampires that might be there. And you'd be able to see them."

Splitting up made sense. It would keep Ness in the dark about what we were doing. But there was no way that I was going to be the one to stay here on the boring part of the task. I had to use my head. "Sure. Let me feed on you. That way our connection will be stronger."

It was small, but I could see Christian shudder, and I could hear his heart speed up. Not one time since Atlantic City had he allowed me to feed on him directly. Christian tolerated our connection, but he didn't like it. Was I being a *tokhes* to get what I wanted? Hell, yes.

It's what you usually do, Sarah said.

You shouldn't act like that, Mom scolded. *I raised you better.*

He's your partner, and he deserves your respect, Dad added.

I know, I know, I just can't stand by doing nothing, I replied.

"Fine. You go." He turned to me. "But just observe and gather information. Don't start anything!"

The last words were shouted to me, as I'd already jumped out of the car and was heading to the station to catch the L.

Chapter 5

It had stopped raining as I rode the L north and got off at Logan's Square. The day was warm for mid-March, and the rain-slicked sidewalks were creating a thin mist that hugged the ground. I had to walk down Kedzie Boulevard for a few blocks before turning down a side street.

Pandora's Legacy pool hall was on the ground floor of a tenement midway down the block. The door was set back from the front of the building, and stenciled on the glass in gold block letters was the name "E.M. Craig" with "Proprietor" underneath.

Cigar and cigarette smoke wafted out as I pushed open the door, along with another smell that took me a moment to place—pickled herring. The room was barely big enough to have four pool tables squeezed into the space, as long as you didn't mind your cue teasing the backside of the players at the other tables. The room was dimly lit along the perimeter, but each table was starkly bathed in light from hanging lamps. Booths lined the near wall, and a bar ran along the opposite wall. A large radio playing big band music stood along the back wall. It sounded like Earl Hines.

Four men were playing at two of the tables, with two players at each one; the other two tables were not occupied. Two men, each with a dame leaning on them, stood at the bar. There was a soft thump as cue hit ball, and a click as the ball hit a second ball, kissing it gently and sending it into a side pocket. It was the only sound in the room (other than the big band music coming from the radio) as all conversation had stopped when I entered.

The shooter who'd made the shot stood up and leaned against his cue, while the other three players all stared at me, casually holding their own cues. I didn't feel any tingling sensation, so all of the people present were human.

But could they be like this Renfield person, like your partner? Dad asked.

I gave him a mental shrug. I had no way of knowing if they were or not.

One of the men at the bar drained his pint of beer, setting the glass on the counter. He stood up, the dame sliding off his arm like water off a bronze statue. The man wasn't tall—about my height—but he was barrel-chested, and his arms were as thick as my thighs. He had blond hair and a blond mustache and beard.

"We don't get many Jews up here." His voice was deep and had a pronounced Norwegian accent. "This is a private club."

It was a veiled threat, and I could see the players all grip their cues a bit tighter. "I'm looking for Craig."

"I'm Eric Craig," said the barrel-chested man. He took a few steps toward me, walking between the tables. "You must be a cop, asking dumb questions like that."

"I'm not a cop," I said, gauging the tension in the room. "I'm looking for work."

Craig barked a laugh and turned to his friends.

"Hear that? Our Jew here must think I'm somebody important." He stuck his thumbs into his suspenders and puffed out his chest. "Do I look like Mayor Thompson to you? Handing out jobs to every *schmo* that walks in the door?" His friends laughed, and Craig gave me a predatory smile.

"Some guys I met said that there was work here for people who aren't afraid to get their hands dirty."

"There's a clogged toilet in the back," laughed one of the players. "I'll pay you a buck to go clean it out." The others joined in the laughter.

I was tired of this, so I looked Craig in the eyes. "Two men shot up Capone's car the other day. They were hired by a man from your pool hall. A man in brown. Tell me who hired these men." I put as much persuasion behind the command as I could. I really didn't know how this power worked; it was like equal parts persuasion, hypnotism, and my own will. But I didn't need to know *how* it worked, just that it *did* work.

Except when it doesn't, teased Sarah.

Shit. Craig was laughing again, his hand casually playing with a billiard ball on the table, spinning it, letting it thump against the bumper. I could see the edge of some kind of braided bracelet around his wrist.

"I knew you was a cop. And a dumb cop, at that. No guys were hired from my place to shoot up Capone. One, we ain't that stupid. And two..."

"Capone'd be in a grave instead of livin' it up downtown," concluded one of the pool players. They were all spreading out now, moving to try to circle me. I could hear their hearts starting to beat faster.

They are beneath you, Saul, Moira's voice stated in my head. *They think they can take you. But they don't know who they are dealing with.*

I balled my hands into fists.

Fighting is never the answer, Dad chided.

Don't listen to him. I could hear the pout in Moira's voice. *They need to be taught a lesson. You're one of the Blessed. They need to know their place.*

Craig was still talking. "...is going to come in here and order me around."

They all moved as one, much faster than I expected. Craig picked up the ball and hurled it at me, while the other five men rushed me. The ball was aimed at my head, and I jerked to the right fast enough that it sailed past. I heard it smack into the wall, and I saw Craig's eyes widen just a bit.

He didn't expect that.

His two friends on my flanks swung their pool cues at my head, and two others aimed their cues at my stomach. They must have done this before, as they were very coordinated and didn't interfere with each other's attacks. The fifth guy pulled his hand from his coat pocket, and I saw the glint of brass coming from across his fingers.

I made a quick decision. The first two cues hit me in the head—hard—smashing to splinters.

Good thing you have such a hard head, Sarah laughed. *I'm surprised it didn't echo.*

It still hurt!

I grabbed one of the cues that had been aimed toward my midsection in my left hand, and I turned slightly so that the other cue struck my back. I heard a CRACK as it shattered. Before Knuckles could react, I pulled the cue from the man's hands and shoved it into Knuckle's gut. There was a satisfying grunt and he doubled over.

I heard Craig yelling something, but I couldn't understand his... Swedish? Norwegian?

Don't think, Saul! Urged Moira. *Kill them!*

I hadn't realized that my fangs had extended. Each of the men was reacting to what I'd done, and maybe to Craig's shouts. The two who'd hit me in the head pulled the broken cues back and tried to stab at me, aiming for my chest.

I swung my cue, swinging it like a baseball bat at the two men on my left. I hit the first man in the head, and he fell back, dazed. The other ducked to avoid the blow, but that messed up his jab with his makeshift stake.

Then I cursed, *"Kuck ind fall!"* as the other cues stabbed me. I'd turned in my swing, so one hit my back, and the other hit my arm. But blood still flowed.

That looks like it hurt, Sarah commented.

You're not helping!

End this, Moira said. *Feast on their blood.*

Also not helping! But she was right. I had to end this soon. Knuckles had recovered, and I still had to deal with Craig.

And four pissed off Swedes, said Sarah.

Norwegians.

Whatever.

I jumped up, landing on the table of one of the booths behind me, and then kicked hard at the first man who tried to stab me. My foot connected with his jaw, and blood and a tooth flew as he went down. I managed to block another stab at me with my own cue, and then jumped again, leaping over the men and landing on one of the pool tables. I turned to face the four men who were just now turning. Then my head exploded in pain as a pool ball hit me.

I turned and snarled at Craig, and he stared back, unconcerned by the monster in his pool hall. He threw another ball, but I was ready and swung the cue, sending the ball flying to the back of the room. Roger Hornsby couldn't have hit it better.

Stop holding back, Saul, Moira said. *Don't play with your food.*

I'm not going to kill them!

They don't seem to have the same idea, Sarah noted.

I thrust my cue at the nearest man, shoving it into his shoulder. He gave a cry as I pulled it out and swung at his head. He dropped like a rock.

Two down.

I jumped down from the table as another pool ball flew past where my head had just been. I swung at one of the men as another tried to stab me. I connected, causing the man to see stars, but the other cue stabbed my arm. More blood flowed, and I reflexively opened my hand, my cue falling to the floor. *Damn, my first wounds had just healed, too.*

And the way you're acting, they won't be the last ones you suffer today, Moira replied, impatiently. *Why won't you just kill them?*

I pulled the cue from my arm, and threw a punch at the man's face. My hand connected, and blood spurted from his nose. He staggered, slipped on my fallen cue, and fell backwards, hitting his head on one of the pool tables.

Four down.

And yet, Moira said, *they're all still alive. Somehow. You disappoint me.*

My kidney exploded in pain, and I staggered away from Knuckles. He was babbling at me in Norwegian, and he looked like pictures I'd seen of Viking warriors—minus the horned helmet.

How can you let him get away with that? Moira asked. *You're one of the Blessed. You're superior to these playthings. Start acting like it, and kill him!*

Enough! I screamed at her. *Between his blabbering and yours, I can't even think straight!*

He jabbed with his left, trying to get me to react as he swung hard with his right—and the brass knuckles. I caught the blow in my left hand, which hurt like hell—I think he broke a couple of bones—but his wide eyes and open mouth proclaimed his surprise.

I brought around my right in a strong uppercut that would have made Gene Tunney proud. Knuckles' head jerked back, and I saw his eyes roll back into his head. He dropped like a sack of potatoes.

Five down.

Stars exploded in my eyes as another pool ball hit me.

Forget somebody? Sarah asked.

No, I didn't forget him, damnit!

Moira's disgust with me was clear, as she said, *This has gone on for far too long. None of these insects should have ever laid their hands on you. Finish this!*

My head was still ringing, but my other wounds had already healed. Even my broken hand was feeling almost normal. I was glad I had fed right before we'd begun the stakeout.

I turned and rushed Craig before he could launch any more pool balls. He should have been surprised, as I was moving fast enough that it should have looked to him like I'd just disappeared and then reappeared—like a magician's trick. Instead, he was ready for me, and he flicked open a switchblade just as I was making contact.

The blade slid into my chest, and I could feel it scrape against my ribs. It missed my heart, but it pierced my lung. My anger finally boiled over, and I pushed out with my hands, shoving Craig back with enough force that he flew to the back of the room. He struck the radio, which exploded into hundreds of pieces.

I rushed forward, the knife wound burning in my chest. The only sound in my head was Moira, screaming, *Kill him! Feed!*

I grabbed Craig, lifting his limp body with one hand and, before I knew it, I felt my teeth sinking into his throat.

Chapter 6

The blood was warm and sweeter than any candy. I was suddenly more awake, more 'alive' than ever. I could feel the wounds from my fight healing—the bones in my hand mending, the knife wound knitting itself together.

Yes! Drink! Take his power! Moira was giddy with delight.

The hot liquid glided down my throat, slaking a thirst I'd not realized that I had. My whole body tingled with excitement, with pleasure. Then, all too soon, it was over. No more blood flowed, despite my trying to get more out.

I broke my grip and dropped the lifeless body to the floor. I was shocked to find that there was practically no blood on Craig's body. I wiped my mouth, and only a tiny bit of blood smeared my hand. I quickly licked it, not wanting to waste any of the precious liquid.

What in the hell did you do? Sarah's voice was accusatory and scared.

He did what he was reborn to do. Moira's own voice was harsh, but pleased.

Oy vey! Dad's voice chimed in. *You could have done that to your partner.*

No wonder he's so scared of you, Mom had to add.

I took several steps back, leaning against a pool table. I suddenly felt sick to my stomach. Yes, I'd fed on

Christian, but not like this, and every time since that first time in Atlantic City, he'd given me his blood in a cup. I'd not fed on him directly. I'd never fed on another human. I'd never killed anybody.

I'm a murderer! My stomach lurched, and I couldn't hold it back any longer. I vomited Craig's blood all over the floor.

Suck it up, Saul, Moira said, disgusted with me. *You've finally become what I wanted you to become.*

I'm a monster, I thought. I heard mumbled agreement from my family.

No! Moira yelled. *This was unavoidable. You were destined to become one of the Blessed. You have a powerful gift. Embrace it. Use it. Do some good with it.*

I always said, never start a fight, Dad said. *But if you must fight, fight to win.*

When did you ever say that last part? I asked.

Feh, I've always believed that.

Well, I won. It doesn't feel like it, though. Not when the loser is dead on the floor.

He was a schmuck, Sarah said. Both Mom and Dad scolded her.

It's true, Sarah argued. *And how did he beat all of your fancy vampire gifts anyway?*

Yeah, how did *he resist me? He was fast, too.*

I stepped back to the body and started searching his pockets. Other than a wallet and some keys, he didn't have anything unusual on him. Then I remembered something, and looked at his wrist. He wore a braided leather bracelet, which seemed odd to me. A few ivory-looking beads were tied into the braid. It was a strange choice for jewelry, but maybe it was a Norwegian thing.

I stood up, realizing that I hadn't learned anything about who had hired the gunmen to shoot at Capone. *Man, Christian is going to kill me. Literally, if he finds out what I've done.*

The other men were still alive, but I doubted that they knew anything. They were followers, and it was unlikely that they'd be able to tell me anything useful. I looked around for the two dames, and I realized that, at some point, they had fled, probably during all the fighting.

Shit. I was not looking forward to telling Christian that we had *bupkis.*

As I was turning to leave, I stopped. I'd just heard a voice. No, not a voice. A laugh. Somebody had laughed. It had been faint, but it had come from behind the bar. Or was it just something in my head?

Wasn't us, said Sarah.

I went to the bar and listened. My senses felt like they'd been hooked up to a power station. I heard *everything.* Leaking pipes. The ticking of a clock. The scratching of rats.

Maybe it was nothing?

There. I heard it again. A voice, though it was muffled, indistinct. I couldn't make out the words, but it was clearly a voice. Raised in anger? I looked down, as it seemed that the voice had come from the floor. I didn't see anything other than sawdust, spilled beer, and pieces of a pool cue. I remembered the night at the Green Mill, when I'd followed Jack McGurn out of the speakeasy when the cops had raided the place. He'd had a tunnel under the bar.

Capone's escape tunnel, Moira said.

I started looking around for a switch or anything

that would open a trapdoor. Nothing. Then I saw a plain wooden box sitting on the top shelf, right where someone would stand to draw beers from the tap. On the front was painted the word "Pandora".

Clever. I tried to move or open the box, but nothing happened. Then I saw a keyhole in the top. I went back and grabbed the keys from Craig's body. It only took a couple of tries to find the right key, and the box opened. Inside was a switch.

Remembering my fall into the tunnel under the Green Mill, I flipped the switch, careful not to fall in case the door was right under me. This time, a section of floor near the back wall dropped down, creating a ramp. When I approached, I saw that the floorboards had rotated to create steps, and a ladder had slid out of the end. A dim light bulb cast a feeble glow.

I glanced back, wondering if I should deal with the other men. They were still out cold, so I took the keys and locked the front door, and then moved the bodies so that nobody could see them if they looked in a window. I didn't need the cops, or any of their friends, showing up unannounced.

I returned to the top of the hidden stairs.

And what makes you think that anybody down there knows anything? Dad asked.

Because only bad guys hide out in secret cellars.

Chapter 7

The ladder led down into a concrete cellar that was filled with barrels of beer and crates of whiskey. I pulled out one of the bottles and recognized a Canadian brand. So not only were they hooked up with Mr. Brown (yeah, I didn't have any proof of that—yet), they were bootleggers as well.

The cellar was damp and musty, and I started to think that I hadn't heard any voices at all. Then a raised voice reached my ear. It came from behind a bookcase that was filled with junk. As I stepped up to it, I could feel the faintest of breezes.

It only took me a moment to find the release—a knothole in the upper right corner that was actually a button—and opened the secret door.

Wow, Sarah said. *An actual secret door. It's like something out of Treasure Island.*

There wasn't a secret door in Treasure Island, I told her.

So? It's still cool.

It's just a secret door.

And how many of those have you ever come across? Sarah huffed. I could picture her folding her arms and glaring at me. I looked into the space behind the door. It was pitch black, but my eyes allowed me to see clearly enough.

Ooh... more stairs, Sarah said. I couldn't tell if she was mocking me or not.

I chose to ignore her and headed down. The stairs were made of brick, as were the walls and vaulted ceiling. I had to tread lightly in order to not make any noise. A sudden sound from the bottom of the stairs told me that any sound that I made here would carry. The sound I heard had clearly been a slap to someone's face.

"I... deserve..."

The voice was clearer, though it was still distorted, even to my ears. I continued down the stairs as fast as I could without making any noise. I don't know if it was Bram Stoker's fault or somebody else's, but the dead are not quiet. We make just as much noise as the next person. Especially in an underground brick tunnel.

"Yes, you did."

I paused partway down the stairs. That had been a woman's voice. And had there been a grunt, too?

I continued and finally reached the bottom of the stairs. I was in another small cellar with one door ahead and another to my right. To my left was another set of stairs going up, maybe to the street, or to another building. The door ahead of me was closed tight, its hinges looking rusted, but the one on my right was open a crack, a yellow light spilling into the cellar.

"Stop, please," the first voice struggled to say. It sounded strained, but it was male. I moved a bit closer. Somebody cleared their throat.

"I don't regret what happened, but it was wrong of me to act alone."

My eyes widened and my heart stopped beating. A thousand shivers ran up my spine. The last time that I'd heard that voice was in Atlantic City last year.

Mr. Brown.

I wonder what he's doing down here? Moira asked.

My heart was racing faster than the cars at the Indy 500, and I felt myself tense up. It took a moment for me to realize that I didn't *feel* Mr. Brown. I was sure that I was close enough that we should be able to feel each other's presence. *Why not?*

"You acted like an impulsive child," the woman said. "And I paid the price."

Her voice sounded familiar, but I had trouble placing it. This has to be Brown's master—the mysterious woman who'd been tweaking Capone's nose.

And looking out for you, added Dad.

Yeah, Saul, Moira pouted. *Who is this mysterious woman? Tell me so I can rip out her throat in a jealous rage.*

I don't know who it is! And I don't know why she's been interested in me.

Why would any woman be interested in you? Sarah had to add.

"Did you stop to think that she would find out what you did? Did you bother to think that she'd take her anger out on me?" The woman's voice was angry and irritated and, deep down, I was pleased that Mr. Brown was getting a tongue lashing.

"This doesn't involve her," Brown insisted. "This was between you and Capone."

"It wasn't part of her plan, and that makes it her business."

Who are they talking about? Does Brown's master have her own master?

"But we want the same thing." I could hear the frustration in Brown's voice.

"Yes, we do."

Was that resignation?

"And we'll get our revenge, but it has to be on her terms. That was the deal."

There was definitely resignation in the woman's voice now, and the familiarity continued to tickle at my memory.

"That damn deal," Mr. Brown said, clearly angry. "She's just using you. Using us. She doesn't care what you want, only that she can get you to do her shit work."

"I'm only here because of her. I still don't know how this works, but I cannot refuse her." There was a pause, and then she said, "Maybe I should blame you, since you made the deal with her."

"I should have never taken you to that bitch, but I couldn't bear the thought of losing you like that."

"You did what you thought was the best for me." There was a pause, and I could make out the sound of a hand patting a cheek. "I would never blame you for what happened. This is all their fault."

Whose fault? What happened? Damnit, why can't they just speak clearly?

Yeah, Sarah agreed, *why won't the bad guys explain themselves openly so that even a* nudnik *like you can understand?*

"If doing Kalfu's dirty work means that I can get my revenge on them, then all of this will be worth it," the woman said.

Kalfu? Was this another vampire? Was she the woman's true master? How far does this go?

"And when I've gotten my revenge," the woman continued, "then we can see how far Kalfu's influence over me goes. I don't plan on being in that witch's control any longer than I have to, but none of that will be possible if you continue to pull stupid stunts like you did with Capone."

"It wasn't a stunt. Kalfu doesn't understand how things are done in Chicago," Mr. Brown said.

Damnit, I need to get closer. This was great information, but it would be worthless if I couldn't find out who Brown was talking to. I slowly started to inch toward the door.

"For now, she's in charge. Remember that."

"Fine," Brown practically spat the word, "so she wants to be in control? Then she needs to learn how Chicago operates. Capone needed to be sent a message. He thought he was untouchable in that cozy jail cell, and we had to show him that we could have gotten to him at any time. You spent time with that bastard. You, of all people, know how Capone thinks. How he reacts."

What? Brown's boss had been with Capone? That didn't make any sense to me.

"It was still a stupid move. Yes, Capone needed to be sent a message, but, by acting alone, you managed to piss Kalfu off. Had we approached her the right way, and explained things, she might have let us send the message the proper way, and she wouldn't be mad at me. Now she doesn't trust me. She's afraid that she cannot control me, so that means that she's going to try to exert even more control. That will make it harder for me to do what needs to be done, and harder for me to get away from her when she's finished with her plans. Your stunt has put everything at risk."

I continued to inch forward. I could almost see into the room. I still didn't know why I couldn't feel Mr. Brown or the mysterious woman, but if I couldn't feel them, then the opposite had to be true.

Yeah, right, sneered Sarah. *You are the vampire expert, after all.*

"With one impulsive decision, you could have made all of my sacrifices worthless," the woman said.

I could see into the room now through a slight crack between the door and the wall. All I could make out was the slender, pale arm of the woman. If she'd just move a little bit, I might—

Suddenly, the woman moved, and the door was pulled open. The room was lit by a single dim overhead bulb, but it was bright enough to make my eyes blink at the sudden change in brightness.

"Hello, Saul," the woman purred. "Fancy meeting you here."

Chapter 8

"Don't be rude, Saul. If you keep your flap open, a fly will get in." She stroked her finger under my chin and a tingling started in my loins and ran up my back. I closed my mouth, still in shock.

"Moira?" I asked, stunned.

That's not *me*, the Moira in my head stated, emphatically.

I couldn't reconcile the vision and voice of the Moira in my head with the person standing before me. She looked like Moira, but she was... different. She wore a black dress with short sleeves and a hem that fell to just above her knees. The dress was trimmed in red, which only served to show just how much that her once-brilliant red hair had faded. Moira had been pale when we'd dated—I'd assumed that it was from being the dead of winter in Chicago, but it was really because she had been dead—but now her skin looked even worse. It was ashen, and there were deep hollows in her cheeks and around her eyes.

Despite these changes, she still had a figure to die for, and her green eyes were vibrant, piercing me with their gaze. I felt my heart race and my mouth go dry.

"Moira?" I repeated.

Oh, please, the Moira in my head sulked. *She looks so—*

"You look dead," I blurted out.

I saw Mr. Brown's mouth twitch into a scowl, but Moira—*was it really her?*—merely laughed, a sound that was somehow both familiar and foreign to me.

"Oh, Saul. Still as blunt as always." She turned and stepped into the room. It had meager furnishings: a table and some chairs, a ratty looking couch, and an armchair that looked remarkably clean. Moira sat on the couch, crossing her legs and patting the spot next to her. "Come have a seat, Saul. We've so much to catch up on."

I took a hesitant step into the room. Mr. Brown threw a look at Moira, then pulled out a chair at the table and slouched down into it, glaring at me.

I chose the armchair. For the briefest of moments, I saw something flicker across Moira's expression. *Approval? Anger?*

Chagrin, my Moira said.

"I'm so glad we ran into each other," Moira said. "Ever since last year, I've been so worried about you. But look at you now," she ran her eyes up and down my body, and I felt like I was being sized up to be butchered. "All grown up and no longer a Vegan." Another turn of her lips.

Pride?

Disappointment, my Moira corrected me.

"But," I stammered out, licking my lips. They had suddenly gone dry, despite the moisture in the cellar. "The last time we saw each other, you tried to kill me."

"And you broke my heart, Saul." She put a hand to her chest. "With a chair leg. But that's all water under the bridge. I don't blame you for what you did."

"You don't?" I seemed to recall the event differently.

46

Yeah, Moira said in my head. I could hear the anger and resentment. *I said you were a fucking waste of my time. You were so disappointing.*

"I thought you said that I had been a disappointment," I said, looking down at my shoes. "That I was a waste of your time."

Another tinkle of laughter came from Moira. It sounded out of place, coming from her. "Of course not, Saul. You were never a disappointment to me. And the fact that you're here, now, proves my point."

"It does?" *I'm confused.*

That's not a stretch, both Sarah and Moira said in my head.

"You've proven yourself, proven to me that you were the right choice all along. What I did—what I was forced to do—last year? That was all Capone. He made me do it. You know what he's capable of. He's a monster.

"He forced me to attack you. And what you did?" She placed her hand on my arm, and I felt a jolt of excitement run up my arm and straight to my heart. "It was only natural for you to defend yourself. I don't blame you for that. I never wanted to hurt you." Her fingers traced down my arm and then gave my hand a gentle squeeze. The feel of her hand brought back memories of fun and laughter in speakeasies, but then there was a sharp, cold burn. I looked and finally noticed that she wore a leather bracelet, with small white stones woven into it. It burned and hurt where it touched me, but Moira's grip was like a vise, and I couldn't pull my hand away.

"I was compelled to attack you by Capone. You know how he always has to get his way. You know his power."

I nodded, remembering the dreadful night when he'd "invited" me into my neighbor's apartment. I'd been unable to resist his command. I'd been unable to stop him from slaughtering my neighbor.

Moira finally released my hand and I pulled it to my chest, the cold burn still tingling even as the wound healed. She gestured to Mr. Brown, her long fingers and red nail polish turning the simple gesture into something seductive. "If I'd wanted to hurt you, I wouldn't have had Brian looking out for you, now would I?"

Brian? That seemed like such an ordinary name to me. "You could have fooled me. The last time we met, he tried to rip my head off."

Mr. Brown—Brian—flashed me a smile that was more fang than humor. I felt like a sheep being stared at by a wolf. I turned back to Moira, but the feeling didn't quite go away.

"But I thought you died. Why didn't you come see me? Why didn't you come and talk to me instead of always sending *Brian* to watch me?"

"No, Saul. I didn't die." Moira crossed her arms and started to tease the leather bracelet. "You got lucky with the chair leg, but I didn't die. It just took me a while to get over it."

Did she mean get over the injury, or the fact that I had defied her? Ruined her plan?

"I had to plan how I was going to get back at Capone for what he's done to me. What he's done to both of us. I am strong, Saul, but even I can't take on Capone alone. Our little spat was proof of that."

Spat? Sarah said. *I'd hate to see what happens when she gets really angry.*

"And I wasn't sure if you wanted to see me again. I was afraid that you'd blame me for everything."

"Why would I blame you?"

What, she attacks you in your home, and that would just be water under the bridge? Dad asked.

Capone ordered her to do that, I replied.

Oh, and that little love bite she gave you meant nothing? Do you think that was on Capone's orders, too? Sarah asked.

Well...

Face it, Saul, Sarah added. *She took you for a* putz. *She used you.*

And it was a fucking waste of my time, too, my Moira added.

"But Capone..." I stopped, as I realized that I'd spoken aloud. Moira—the one sitting on the couch—replied before anybody in my head could get a word in.

"Capone is at the center of it all. He's the spider sitting in his web, waiting for the flies to come along. He doesn't care whose life he ruins as long as he gets his way. He made me into *this*. He made me win your heart so that you could be used. And when he had his way, he would have thrown you aside, disposed of you as easily as throwing out the garbage."

She flashed me a smile. "But I saved you from that. I had a plan for you—and I still do."

"A plan for me?"

"We want the same thing, Saul." She looked at me with her green eyes.

"Get Capone," I said. Moira nodded, and patted my knee.

"He needs to be removed from power if any of us ever want to be free."

By using guns and bombs? Dad asked. *Your boss, Ness, he'll do the same thing, but without any of the violence.*

How many innocent people will get hurt if you help

her? Mom asked.

I looked at Moira, stared directly into her pretty green eyes. "We have a plan to get Capone. And we won't need bombs or Tommy Guns to do it. Nobody will get hurt and he'll be put away."

Moira looked at me for a moment, and then laughed. It was meant to mock, to sting. I felt my face blush.

"Do you think Capone will ever let that happen?"

"He just spent—"

"Don't be naïve, Saul. You know he allowed that to happen. Capone only respects power."

"And how many innocent people will get hurt in the process?"

Moira patted my knee again, as if I was a child who'd just said something stupid. "Some of the sheep may get hurt," she shrugged, "but you can't make an omelet without breaking some eggs. A few sacrifices will be worth it if Capone is gone for good. Leaving him in power risks many more lives than those who might get caught in the crossfire. In the end, everything will be better."

"So the ends justify the means?" I asked, tartly. I could taste bile in the back of my throat.

"Saul, don't act like a child. People die every day in this town from the gangs, from petty criminals, from corrupt cops, hunger, exposure, and a hundred other reasons. Sure, a few sheep may die, but the rest will scatter and cower, and we'll be able to take out Capone. The world will be better for it."

"And what about me?"

"If you want to make sure that the sheep are safe, then stay out of my way. I can't have you and your friends bumbling about, sticking your noses into places they don't belong."

"I can't stand aside while you hurt innocent people."

"Nobody in this town is innocent," Brian said, finally breaking his silence. I wanted to argue with him, but I knew it would be pointless.

"Besides, Saul," Moira purred. She traced a red-tipped finger up the side of her neck. "I don't want you getting hurt. Brian will be too busy to save you this time."

"I can take care of myself." I couldn't keep from putting a lot of pride into my statement.

"I've no doubt," she patted my knee. *Why did it feel like I was being acknowledged by Bubby?* My grandmother could make you feel small and insignificant with a pat and a single word.

"I wanted to introduce you to our ways myself. You've done surprisingly well on your own, but you are still a babe in the woods. You don't know the score, Saul, and if you got hurt, I just couldn't live with myself." She gave a small laugh, as if acknowledging the pun she'd just made.

"You mean we could be together?" I asked. "And you could help me understand what I've become?"

"Of course. You've been wandering in the darkness for too long. I can teach you, and it will be just like it was before." She ran her fingers up my thigh.

She's playing you for a sap, my Moira growled in my head. *That's not me. She doesn't love you like I did.*

I hate to agree with the bloodsucker, said Sarah, *but she's right. Something's not right here.*

Where else can I learn everything that I don't know?

Sure, and the woman who tried to kill you is where you should get your answers, Dad said. *You might as well go back to Capone.*

51

That was before.

Before? Before she went into hiding? Before she sent this schmo *to spy on you and try to kill you? You're* meshuga *if you—*

Dad's tirade was lost as Moira leaned close to me, her scent strong and heady, and said, "Promise me that you won't interfere, Saul, and once Capone is dealt with, we can be together. Forever." Then her lips were on mine, and all of the protests in my head were silenced.

Chapter 9

My head was in a fog as I left the pool hall. I could still feel where Moira's lips had touched mine. It had been more than a kiss, more than an intimate touch. It had brought back a flood of memories of the time before all of this. Before the St. Valentine's Day massacre. Before I became a pawn of Capone and Moran. Before I learned that vampires were real.

You mean back when you were just a regular schmuck, Sarah said.

And just because you didn't know it, Dad said, *doesn't mean that she wasn't still a monster. Do you not remember how she was using you?*

I was, Moira added, unapologetically.

I shook my head and headed back to Kedzie Boulevard and Logan Square. Moira was alive.

Undead, Moira corrected, and I shrugged.

She wasn't dead—really dead. *This changes so much.*

I had been a vampire for over a year now, and I had only learned a few things about what I was. I still had a lot of questions, and I had no place to go to for answers. Joe had run away. Capone's offer came with a price I was unwilling to pay. The only thing that Christian knew was how best to kill me. But now I had another choice, and learning from Moira would be so much better than learning from Capone.

And replacing one monster with another is better how? Dad's voice was insistent.

This is different.

No, it's not. Oy! Lord, forgive my son. One kiss by a pretty woman and he's only thinking with his schlong.

I am not! I'm actually thinking with my head.

Feh. Dad was not impressed, and Sarah had to add, *That'd be a first.*

I reached Logan's Square and headed for the L. This would be perfect. Moira would take care of Capone and, in the process, she'd be able to tell me what I needed to know about being a vampire.

And all the innocents? Mom prompted. *Are you willing to let more little girls get blown up?*

I'll watch Moira. I'll keep her in line. She'd told me to stay out of her way, but that was with Capone. If I can stay close to Moira and Brian, I could keep an eye on them.

And what makes you think she'll let you do that? Dad's question hung there as I got on the train.

She just said that she still loved me.

When did she say that? Did you hear that? I didn't hear her say that she loved you. I think you're hearing things as you want them to be, Saul, Dad said.

Well, it's what she meant.

Now you are an expert on women! I could hear the mocking tone from Dad. *Last year you were an expert on being a Federal agent after just a month on the job. Now, you know everything about women? I've been married to your mother for over twenty years, and I don't know women.*

She wants me to be with her.

She tried to kill you.

That was Capone, not Moira.

I'm pretty sure that was me, love, Moira said.

See! Dad insisted. *I know what I'm talking about.*

No, you don't! I gripped the bar over my head tightly as I screamed at Dad. *She didn't* want *to kill me. Capone* ordered *her to do it. She wasn't in control.*

And what did she want you for? Dad's question was like a slap of winter wind from Lake Michigan. I mentally looked to Moira.

That's my secret, she teased.

I shrugged. The reasons didn't matter. I couldn't change what had happened, but I could take advantage of the situation. I got off the L and headed back to the speakeasy that Christian and I were watching. It was after midnight now, and the streets were nearly empty. I wasn't surprised to see that Christian hadn't moved. I gave a wave as I crossed the street and opened the car door.

Christian held the lid of a thermos, steam rising from the coffee inside. My foot hit my own thermos—filled with blood, not coffee—but I wasn't hungry.

"I was wondering if you'd forgotten about me," Christian said. There was only a touch of irritation in his voice. "Did you find anything useful at the pool hall?"

I didn't answer right away. *Do I tell him about Moira?*

He's your partner. Of course you tell him, Dad insisted.

But I know how he'll react if he learns that Moira is still alive.

Undead, Moira added, unhelpfully.

"Well?" Christian prodded. "Was it a dead end?"

"No. The two thugs that shot up Capone's car were hired there. And it was Mr. Brown who did it."

"He was there? Did he see you?" Christian turned in the driver's seat to look at me. "Did you start anything?"

"I didn't start anything." That was enough of the truth that I didn't bother to add any details. "But I did learn who Brown's master is."

I could see Christian's eyes widen. Before he could ask, I said, "It's Moira. She's still alive and she's Brown's master. She's been behind him all along. She's the one gunning for Capone."

"Moira?" I heard his breath catch. "She's not alive."

Did he not hear me right?

"Yes, she is. I *saw* her."

"Oh, I believe you. But she's an undead abomination just like Capone and the others."

Just like you, Saul, Moira cooed.

"She's not alive," Christian stated. "But how did she survive? Truesdale said you drove a chair leg though her heart."

I shrugged. "I don't know, and the subject didn't come up."

Christian raised an eyebrow. "Wait. You spoke with her?"

"Umm… yes?"

Christian put a hand to his face. "What did you two chat about?" he asked through his fingers.

"She's going to take out Capone."

"We knew that. At least we knew that was the goal of Mr. Brown's boss. Knowing that his boss is Moira doesn't change anything."

"It's still her goal, but I think there's someone else. Someone that Moira reports to."

Christian gave me a look that demanded that I tell him more.

"I had a chance to overhear them talking, before they knew that I was there. Moira mentioned somebody else, someone she's being forced to do jobs for. I don't think she likes that fact."

"Another vampire?"

"I don't know."

"And of course it 'didn't come up' in your conversation."

"Hey, I was a bit busy trying to understand how the woman I thought I'd killed was standing in front of me."

"This doesn't change anything. We still need to stop her and Capone. Knowing that it's Moira just puts a name to this mystery boss. Now we know who else we need to deal with."

"Yeah... I sort of promised to stay out of her way."

"Saints above preserve me," Christian intoned, staring through the car's roof. Turning to me, he said, "And why would you do something stupid like that? You've just given a monster free reign to destroy Chicago as she takes down the biggest gangster in the country."

"I have a plan."

Of course you do, Sarah quipped.

He's the expert on plans now, too, Dad added.

"Great. We know how well those always turn out," Christian replied.

I ignored everyone's sarcasm. "She wants me to not interfere, but if I can get close to her, I can keep her in check. I can make sure that she doesn't hurt anybody while she takes out Capone."

"That'll never happen."

"I'm already there. She wants me with her."

"You're forgetting Ness. You know, your boss? He'll never let you do this."

"He doesn't have to know."

"He'll know. And I don't want to lose my job because you have the hots for this undead whore."

I bristled at the words. She'd tried to kill me, and I thought I'd killed her. I didn't love her anymore.

Then why do you keep me around, Saul? Moira asked.

"We can't let this opportunity get away from us," I said. "Even if we don't stay out of her way, we need to keep an eye on her in order to know what they are doing. If we don't, more innocents like that little girl will be killed."

Christian drummed his fingers against the steering wheel. Finally, he said, "You're right. We can't waste this chance."

"Great. I can get—"

"No."

"What? But you just—"

"I don't trust you with her." I opened my mouth to protest, but he continued. "We don't know what sort of power Moira—or her unknown master—may have over you."

"She didn't try anything tonight." I heard a loud *humpf* from Dad, but I ignored him.

"That doesn't mean she won't try it later. Plus, she may hold back or work in secret if you're around. I'll go keep an eye on things."

"Like hell you will!"

Christian stared at me and I realized that I'd put my foot in it. I might have been able to reason with him, but not now.

"If things go south, I'm better equipped to deal with them." My protest sounded lame, even as I said it.

So it wasn't just me, Sarah said.

"I can take care of myself," Christian patted his coat, which I knew contained several anti-vampire weapons. "And I'm willing to let you feed," he added, almost in a whisper, but still clear to me. "Having our bond at its strongest will be good."

I was surprised at Christian's willingness to let me feed. That he initiated the suggestion was a first for us. "What about me?" I asked.

He pointed down. "You stay here, watching the speakeasy. That way Ness won't get suspicious."

"I get to drive?"

"Lord, no! I'll drop you off here." He pointed at the building outside the car. "I'm sure there's a vacant apartment in the building, or you can use the roof. It'll be good anyway if the car is gone so that they don't see it hanging around."

I looked out at the speakeasy. Nobody had entered since I'd returned. A bum lay in the recess of a door down the block. He had a threadbare blanket pulled up, trying to keep the chill out.

I let out a sigh. "Why now?"

"Now what?"

"Why'd Moira let me know now that she was still... around?"

"Don't let that monster get into your head. She's nothing but trouble. She'll soon regret this mistake."

I looked at Christian. "You sound a lot like Truesdale."

He gave a small nod. "I'll take that as a compliment. He was an overbearing, bull-headed, paranoid man, but he was also cautious. We need to take some of his caution to heart."

Chapter 10

Christian dropped me off after lunch the next day to continue our surveillance on the speakeasy. He'd come to my apartment first, where he'd withdrawn some of his blood for me to drink. I noticed, for the first time, that it had a slightly different flavor from the blood that I'd taken from Craig yesterday. My mind had flashed back to Capone's dinner with the vampires and the special "vintage" he'd had them drink. Was there a difference between blood from a procurator, and blood that we took for food? As usual, I didn't know. *Just one more mystery that I might never solve.*

It was a nice spring day, and a lot of people were out and about. I headed into the building across from the speakeasy and made my way to the roof. It was easier than trying to see if the place had a vacant apartment facing the street. Plus, I wanted the freedom of movement that being on the roof afforded me. I found a perch along the edge, set down my thermos, and then moved into a shadow that was being cast by the adjoining building.

One thing I had learned in the past year was that I could practically become invisible if I was given a bit of shadow. Not that I disappeared completely, like in H.G. Wells' story, but I could stand completely still. People's eyes are attracted to movement, so with a bit of shadow and no movement, people tended to just look past me without actually seeing me. I hadn't ever thought about the ability beyond its practical use, but after feeding on Craig, I now wondered if this wasn't an adaptation for a predator.

The afternoon passed uneventfully, with few people entering and leaving the speakeasy. Nobody who looked familiar from the mug shots that I'd poured over yesterday put in an appearance. I did see a couple of people that had visited the place yesterday, so I figured that they must be regulars.

Christian had arrived at the pool hall and had taken up a position so that 'we' could watch the building. That was a sensation that was still hard to get used to. The first time it had happened, I got a horrible feeling of vertigo, and it had resulted in a goon clocking me in the jaw. I was used to the effects now, but it was still an odd sensation.

I could see through Christian's eyes. Anything that he saw, I could also see. It was like a ghost image, or a double exposure on a photograph. I actually saw both places at the same time, and if I moved or turned my head and Christian didn't—or vice versa—then one image moved while the other stayed still, depending on who did the movement. Closing my eyes helped, as then I could only see Christian's view.

We'd also discovered that Christian had control over what I saw. That the ability could be turned off, we'd learned too late. *That had been a trip to the restroom neither of us wanted to repeat.* Now Christian just had to concentrate a bit to send his sight to me. We hadn't tested this ability as much as I had wanted—Christian was always reluctant to let me have any of his blood—but we had learned that, at least within the city limits, there was no problem with the connection. I'd wanted to try it at further and further distances but, so far, Christian hadn't agreed to my experiments.

The sun was setting and the number of regular folks on the street started to dwindle, though the number of people entering the speakeasy picked up. I saw a bum drag himself out of an alley and take up residence in a doorway a few doors away from the speakeasy. Loud voices came from down the street. I saw a quartet of men dressed in shabby overalls and coats. Workers from a mill or factory, I figured, but their swagger and chatter suggested that they were also at least some sort of petty criminals as well. They acted like they owned the street. *The sun goes down, and out comes the riff-raff.* The quartet soon entered the speakeasy.

Another thing that Christian and I had learned was that he could detect my presence in the same way that I could detect other vampires. The same wasn't true for me. I always had a vague sense of where Christian was, but I couldn't *feel* him like I could Capone and Mr. Brown. Christian thought that it was just me that he could detect—we didn't know any other vampires that we could test his ability on—but I was sure that it was any vampire. I was pretty sure that Frank Nitti was a Renfield, and I think he'd detected me in the closet at The Plantation last year. Christian still wasn't sure, but maybe now, with Moira and Brown back in the picture, we could find out.

Why hadn't I felt Moira yesterday? Or Mr. Brown, for that matter?

Because that wasn't me, Moira said.

It was *you,* I told her. *You're just upset that you look like death warmed over now.* I heard a huff from her, but she offered no further insight.

A few streetlights came on, and a car rattled down the road. The darkness didn't bother me, and I could see the bum lying in the dark doorway, as well as somebody staggering out of the speakeasy and down the alley, probably to take a piss.

With the coming night, I risked moving. Nobody on the street would see me up here now. For want of something to do, I opened the thermos and poured myself a cup of blood.

Shit! I spat the blood out. It tasted rancid, like it had spoiled. But that couldn't be the case, as this was a fresh batch that I'd taken from a butcher's shop after we'd returned from Pennsylvania. It shouldn't have gone bad yet. I'd drunk from this same blood yesterday before we'd started our stakeout.

And certainly nothing has happened since then, Dad said.

We watched the speakeasy. I went to the pool hall. I had to fight...

And now the light comes on, Dad said.

Chomp! Chomp! Sarah added, and then made some sucking noises.

Craig had been the first person that I'd ever fed on— fed on and killed. *Had that done something to me?*

What do you think, baby? Moira asked. *You've finally become one of the Blessed—mind, body, and spirit. You're one of us now.*

No! I refused to believe that. I took another drink from the cup. *I am not a monster. I'm nothing like you and the others.* I forced the blood down just to prove my point.

Too late. I wasn't sure if that was Moira, Sarah, or Dad. Maybe it was all three.

I finished off the cow's blood, suppressing the reflex to gag and spit it all back up. I told myself that it was no worse than the worst yak yak or other ersatz whiskey I'd had before and managed to choke it down. *Barely.*

I closed my thermos with a dramatic twist of the lid.

Who do you think you're fooling? Sarah asked.

Shut up. I set the thermos back down and stared at the road, trying to ignore everyone.

Brooding from a roof isn't really your style, Sarah said. *Though maybe if you had a cape that could flutter in the wind...*

I said, shut up! I continued to stare—not brood, stare—at the speakeasy.

A car came down the road, and I could finally get everybody to stay quiet. It was a nicer car than most for this neighborhood, and my interest grew as it pulled to the curb right below me, across from the speakeasy. Then the engine turned off, and the door opened.

Shit! That's Frank Nitti! I pulled back from the edge of the roof. I was at least forty feet up, but I really had no idea if that was far enough. Christian could detect me at about twenty to twenty-five feet, but I didn't know if that was normal or not for a procurator.

Nitti straightened his coat, waited for a truck to pass, and then crossed the road. He hadn't looked up. I let out a breath. (I was still surprised by the little things my body did reflexively, as I didn't need to breathe at all anymore.)

Nitti paused under a lamp, and then approached the speakeasy. *Wait. Nitti is* here, *going into* this *speakeasy?*

The door opened, and Nitti went inside.

Well, Ness wanted connections to Capone. They didn't get much bigger than this.

Unless he's just stopping for a drink, Dad said.

Don't rain on my parade.

Sure, don't listen to me. You're the expert on every-thing. Certainly Mr. Ness will look over anything that might just be coincidence.

But I can't go inside. Ness told us to just watch the place.

Just then, my vision blurred, and another street layered over the one below me. Christian. Through his eyes, I saw a car driving by, with Mr. Brown at the wheel.

Shit. Nitti is here, and now Mr. Brown is going for a drive? I saw Christian pull in behind Brown and start to follow.

Why isn't anything ever easy?

Chapter 11

Don't be a putz, I told myself. Ness only wanted us to watch the place. He told us not to go inside, no matter what. Whether Nitti is here for a drink or on Capone's business, Ness will be interested to know. Ness is playing a long game, so I don't need to rush in there and confront Nitti. And as for Mr. Brown, there are literally hundreds of places that he could be going. Christian will keep an eye on him.

Wow, Saul. Aren't you the cat's pajamas now? Moira said.

I've learned a few things, I admitted, pride filling my thoughts.

Feh, Dad uttered, but since he didn't say anything else, I could tell that he was impressed.

The other agents on Ness's team might still call me a rookie, but I had learned a few things in the past year. Like how to follow instructions.

When you decide that they suit you, Sarah teased.

Just then, I got another flash from Christian. It was the image of a street sign through his cracked windscreen as he drove through an intersection. (Western Avenue and Roosevelt Road.) Christian kept the connection going. He was following a few cars back, turning to follow Brown. Another street sign came into view. (Damen Avenue.)

Wait. That meant Mr. Brown was heading this way. *Why?* Could that just be a coincidence? I only glimpsed another street sign as Christian had to stop suddenly for a traffic light. I saw him pound the steering wheel with his hand.

Ness had told me that, in police work, there are no coincidences. The only conclusion I could make was that Brown was coming here. *But why?*

Dad coughed in my head, and I looked down at Nitti's car. Well, yes, Nitti would be a target for Brown and Moira if they wanted to get to Capone. Not only would it send a strong message to Capone, getting rid of his right-hand man would also help in anything else they were planning.

But how'd they know that Nitti was here? I looked around the street, but the only person who'd been here any length of time—besides me—was the bum in the doorway. *The bum in the doorway!*

I turned to look at him and saw that he was staring intently at Nitti's car. He also had a perfect view of the speakeasy's entrance. He'd have seen Nitti arrive and go inside, and now he was watching to make sure that Nitti hadn't left.

I'll be damned. The bum is a Renfield working for Mr. Brown. I started to wonder if he was the only one, or if it was possible for a vampire to have more than one procurator. It would make an effective spy network if you could swing it.

Then I heard a car, and I looked up the street. I saw headlights turn onto the road, and a car headed toward me. It pulled to a stop behind Nitti's car, and the engine cut off. A moment later, Mr. Brown stepped out. He wore his signature fashion style—brown suit under a brown trench coat—and in his hand was a Tommy Gun with a drum magazine.

Shit.

Brown was going to take out Nitti, and he wanted to be noisy about it. This was going to be the bomb at the diner all over again. Brown didn't care who got in his way, as long as he got Nitti.

I put my foot on the edge of the roof. A lot of innocent lives would be in danger. Then the thought struck me that, if Brown took out Nitti, we might not get the link that Ness needed in order to pin the speakeasy's money to Capone. This could blow any case we might have against Capone out of the water.

Is that his plan? I wondered. *Solve two problems with one attack?* I hesitated for a moment. *But how would Brown and Moira know that we were watching this place?*

It was too complicated for me to think through, and Mr. Brown was crossing the street. I had to do something.

I jumped off the roof of the building, something I'd done before many times, and was startled as I floated down to the ground rather than having one of my usual knee-jarring landings. It was like when Joe had jumped off the roof in front of my parent's place last year. I wanted to enjoy the sensation more, but I had to focus on stopping Mr. Brown.

He was across the street, taking his time and, as I landed, I felt a familiar tingle crawl about the back of my neck. Mr. Brown must have felt it too—so that ability was working now—as he turned around to stare at me. If he was surprised that I was here, he didn't show it. He turned back to the speakeasy, pulling on the weapon's actuator to chamber a round.

I moved quickly, appearing before him in a blink of an eye. He paused, his eyes narrowing at my sudden appearance.

"Be a good pet and get out of my way."

"I won't let you go in there, *Brian*," I said. Despite my newfound strength after feeding on Craig, and having stood up to Brown before, I was sweating bullets.

"You should be a good pet, go home, and mind your own damn business, like Moira told you."

"Where is she?" I asked, playing a hunch. "Does she know that you're here, or are you using your own initiative like you did with Capone?" He didn't answer, which was answer enough for me, but his eyes also narrowed even more.

"Boy, she was really happy with you last time," I continued, piling on the sarcasm. "Maybe I will leave and go tell Moira what you're doing."

Brown's lip curled up in a sneer. "Go ahead, pet. By the time you tell her, it'll be a done deal."

Yeah, he's scared now. Nice job, nudnik, Sarah taunted.

"Look, *Brian*," I began. His sneer turned to a frown, and I heard a growl that came from deep in his throat. *OK, don't call the vampire holding the machine gun Brian anymore.* "I don't care about Nitti or Capone. But if you go in there, guns blazing, a lot of innocent people will get hurt. I won't let that happen."

"Nobody in Chicago is innocent," he said, echoing what he'd said yesterday. "Certainly no one at a speakeasy. Just consider me a helpful citizen, enforcing the law, like you and your boss. I'm protecting the city from the dangers of rumrunners and bootleggers."

I flashed back to the four men who I'd seen earlier.

Their swagger had spoken volumes. They weren't innocent, that's for sure, but that didn't mean they needed to get cut down in Brown's desire to send a message to Capone.

"We don't go around shooting up speakeasies. Nobody in there deserves to die just because you want to hurt Capone," I said.

Brown gave a chuckle and held his hands out, Tommy Gun pointed at the sky. "So stop me, *pet*."

I hesitated. *Why does he keep calling me 'pet'?*

He waggled the gun a bit. "Well?"

Moira will be mad if I stop him. But the—

I never completed my thought. Searing hot pain erupted from my genitals as Mr. Brown's foot connected with my groin. Getting kicked in the balls hurts. A lot. But getting kicked in the balls by a vampire was a million times worse. I was lifted off the ground, and I fell to the sidewalk like a rag doll.

"That's payback for what you did last year." He spat on the ground where I lay. I watched him walk past me through tear-filled eyes.

"Stay out of this, pet. It doesn't concern you. If you can't get that through your thick Kike skull, I will kill you."

"Moira won't like that," I managed to wheeze. I was already healing from the kick, but the pain still lingered.

"I'm willing to risk the consequences." He pulled open the door and headed into the speakeasy.

I staggered to my feet, swaying a bit as I stood up. I heard a car pull up, and I turned to see Christian's car stop at the curb. He jumped out, his coat flapping behind him.

"What happened to you?"

"Just a bit of payback from our friend. He went inside." I jerked my thumb at the door. "He's gunning for Nitti, but a lot of innocents will get hurt in the process."

"Ness told us to stay out of there."

Just then, there was the distinctive chatter of a machine gun, loud enough that even Christian heard it.

"Ness be damned," I said, rushing to the door.

Chapter 12

The inside of the speakeasy was smoky and dimly lit. Customers were diving under tables or running for any place that was out of the line of fire. One man lay dead by the door, his throat torn out.

Brown stood inside the room, his Tommy Gun pointed at the bar. There had been a mirror behind it, but it had already been shattered. At that moment, a man behind the bar stood up, a Tommy Gun in his hands. He aimed at Brown, but before he could pull the trigger, flame erupted from Brown's own weapon. The man at the bar fell as several bullets struck his chest.

Brown laughed as he sprayed bullets across the bar. From the doorway, I could see a woman in a blue dress cower behind an overturned table. She was right in his line of fire.

I ran at full speed, grabbing the woman and pulling her out of the way, just as the bullets chewed up the table. She screamed at the top of her lungs, possibly from nearly dying, or the horrible sound of gunfire, or maybe it was the sudden surprise of appearing five feet away from where she'd been. I didn't care. Her screams meant that she was alive.

Mr. Brown turned to the back of the room. Another gun had fired, a bullet tearing through his coat. The Tommy Gun in his hands spat more lead and, before I could react, the gunman and two innocents—a man and a woman—fell to the fusillade.

Damnit, they're dead because of me! Because I couldn't stop Brown outside. The anger at my mistake burned a hole in my stomach. I gave a yell and charged at Brown.

I ran like Red Grange running for a touchdown, dodging around tables and people. I was moving so fast that I don't think anybody could see me. Just before I reached him, Brown turned around and brought up the butt of the Tommy Gun. It connected with my jaw, and I spun a complete circle from the blow. A tooth flew from my mouth, and I grabbed a chair to stop my spin.

Ooh... Sarah taunted, *he's stopped short of the goal line!*

Without pausing, I picked up the chair and smashed it into Brown's side. The chair shattered into kindling, a piece digging across his face. I was pleased to see his blood flowing. I became less pleased as I saw the wound heal in the blink of an eye.

I was so focused on the scratch that I failed to see the punch. Brown's fist connected with my face, and I was lifted off the ground and thrown back at least five feet. Blood filled my mouth and, as I spat it out, another tooth came with it.

Shit. If this keeps up, I'll need dentures to finish this fight.

Sarah laughed in my head. *A vampire with false teeth? Now that's* really *scary.*

I got to my knees and wiped my hand across my mouth. It came away red, though I could already feel new teeth coming in. I looked up just as another burst of gunfire echoed in the speakeasy. Another man had fallen at the back of the room—one of the four toughs who I'd seen entering the place earlier in the night.

Movement from a doorway caught my eye, and I saw Frank Nitti pulling out a gun. *If he buys it here, not only will Capone be angry, but so will Ness.*

Brown must have also seen Nitti, as he brought his Tommy Gun around. Again, I didn't hesitate, but this time, I was smart enough to not charge in. Instead, I grabbed the edge of a small cocktail table and flung it toward Brown.

The Tommy Gun barked.

The table wobbled awkwardly and winged Brown.

The bullets chewed up the door frame and wall around Nitti, but none hit him.

Before Brown could do anything else, I ran forward and ripped the gun from his grip, the hot barrel burning my hands. Brown tried to hold onto the weapon, his face a mask of anger, his fangs extended.

Then there was more gunfire—to me it sounded like Christian's .45—but nothing was aimed at us. It had apparently startled Brown, as I took possession of the Tommy Gun. Brown swung his fist at me, and I brought up the weapon in time to block his punch. The submachine gun shattered in my hands.

The sharp staccato of gunfire continued to ring out, and I swear that I saw a bullet pass before my eyes. I didn't have time to be scared. Brown threw more punches, and I did my best to imitate Jack Dempsey. Brown was a fiend, his forehead so furrowed that it looked like it had swallowed his eyes. His anger consumed him. There was no banter. No comments. He was focused solely on killing me.

All of my energy was put to blocking his blows. I could feel bruises forming and healing with each impact. I took a shot to my ribs, feeling several of them crack under the pummeling. I tried to lash out, kicking and kneeing him, but my own attacks were feeble, like a kitten trying to attack a bulldog. *Why can't I fight him? I fed on a man yesterday. I should be stronger than this.*

Well, you did throw it all back up, Moira stated, clearly disappointed in me.

Then I felt a hand like a vise close over my throat, and I was lifted off the ground. I tried to pry Brown's fingers off of my neck as a feeling of déjà vu came over me.

"You have been more trouble than you're worth," he spat. "I should have killed you in the garage last year."

I couldn't get any air to reply, and I couldn't get any purchase on the floor.

"Time to correct my mistake."

Then I was flying backwards across the room. Pain exploded across my back as I crashed through the bar. I hit the wall and fell to the floor, what had remained of the mirror landing around me.

I looked up and saw Brown grabbing a chair leg, ripping it off to make a stake. I knew how this would end, and I wasn't going to let him do to me what I'd done to Moira.

Good idea, Sarah said. *You know, not dying?*

I put my hand out and felt metal. In a single motion, I pulled the Tommy Gun from the dead barman and got to my knees. I took an extra moment to bring the weapon to my shoulder—just as I'd seen Cloonan and the others do during training—as Brown rushed me. He was nearly touching the barrel when I pulled the trigger.

A Tommy Gun has a horrible kick to it, but I was prepared. Plus, Brown was so close that it was impossible for me to miss. The bullets ripped into Brown. He continued forward, driven by anger and momentum. I let him bowl me over, but I kept the trigger pulled as I rolled onto my back. Too quickly, the weapon stopped firing as the drum emptied.

I was coated in blood and, even though I had unloaded the entire magazine into Brown, I was afraid that he'd get up. I scrambled out from under his body, pointing the gun at him even though I had no more bullets.

Out of the corner of my eye, I saw Christian step up, his .45 pointed at Brown's body. I was suddenly aware that the room had gone quiet. I could hear sirens in the distance.

"I think you got him," Christian said.

I pulled open his coat and pulled out the wooden stake that I knew would be there. I then went over to Mr. Brown and plunged the stake through his heart.

"Yeah, I got him."

Chapter 13

"What the hell is this? You were supposed to watch the damn place, not turn it into Swiss cheese." Eliot Ness stood in the speakeasy's doorway, hands on hips, his trench coat open. Cloonan and Friel had arrived with Ness, and he'd sent them outside to deal with the crowd.

"God damnit," he went on, barely pausing for breath. Christian winced, but remained silent. "It's hard enough to run this investigation, but now I've got to fend off both the police and the press. Do you have any idea how fucking hard it is to do that?"

Christian and I kept quiet at the rhetorical question. After Brown had died, most of the people who were still alive and unhurt had fled. There wasn't anything that we could do to stop them. Besides Brown, there had been six other bodies in the speakeasy, and we'd left them where they had fallen, though Christian had found some tablecloths that he had draped over their heads.

For me, the smell of fresh blood was nearly over-whelming. The rank taste of the cow's blood was still on my mind, and it took all of my willpower to not feed on the corpses. It helped that I knew that Christian would put a stake through my own heart if I tried anything like that.

My hunger either put steel in my backbone or addled my brain, because I said to Ness, "We didn't choose to do this. Mr. Brown showed up—"

Addled it is, Sarah said.

"And why in the hell were you even following Mr. Brown?"

"We weren't following him," Christian said, lying so well I think he could have fooled the Pope. Not that he would have tried. "He just showed up here."

Ness glared at us from under the brim of his fedora. Before he could question what Christian had said, I stood up. "He showed up carrying a Tommy Gun. We'd seen Nitti show up earlier, and I knew that Brown was going to take him out. I also knew that would be bad for our case, not to mention all of the innocent lives that might get caught in the crossfire."

"I told you to leave Brown and Nitti alone. You were just supposed to watch the place."

"Damnit," I blurted, unable to control myself. "We can't control what Brown or Nitti do, and I wasn't going to let innocent people get hurt."

Ness looked at the bodies that littered the floor. "Yeah, you did a real bang-up job with protecting these people. Besides, everybody here was breaking the law. Anybody who came here knew what they were getting into."

I let my mouth fall open. "You sound just like Brown and Moira," I pointed to Brown's body.

"Moira?" Ness cocked his head at me.

Oops, Moira said. *Looks like the cat's out the bag.*

"She's alive." I shot a glance at Christian to shut him up. I wasn't in the mood for semantics tonight. "And she is—was—Brown's master."

Ness took a moment to process this, and then waved

it away. "It doesn't matter. I don't want you going near her, either. This case is complex enough, and I don't need you making more of a mess of it by bringing your ex-girlfriend into the mix."

This tasty little morsel has the nerve to tell you to not mess things up? Moira asked.

Sarah added, *Yeah, you don't need any help doing that.*

"Mess things up? Moira and Brown are gunning for Capone, and they don't care who gets caught in the middle. Christian and I did good tonight. We saved lives."

"Damnit, Saul, I don't pay you to save lives. If that's what you want to do, then go join the Coast Guard or something." He jabbed a finger to the floor. "I have just one chance to try to nab Capone, and that involves being patient and collecting evidence. Our job is not to stop every goon that tries to take him out. We can't interfere, and some innocent people may get hurt that way, but that's the price we pay to be able to put Capone behind bars."

My stomach tightened and I clenched my fists. *Who's the damn monster now?* I was getting tired of all of this, and I was about to tell Ness just that, when Christian put his hand on my shoulder. He'd been quiet, but now he stepped forward, holding something out to Ness.

"Had Saul and I not intervened, we wouldn't have found this."

"What is it?" Ness asked, taking the item and looking at a bloodstain on it. I could see that it was a large book of some kind.

"Nitti was carrying that when Mr. Brown tried to perforate him. He dropped it in the excitement, and I managed to persuade him to leave it on the floor. Nitti fled out the door with the others, but he left that behind."

Ness opened the book, thumbing through the pages. His eyes widened, and I could hear his heartbeat pick up.

"I think it's a ledger," Christian said. "A *real* ledger," he gave me a sideways look, "that shows payments to people from this speakeasy. Maybe others."

"Including Capone." It wasn't a question from Ness, but Christian demurred.

"Probably. It's in code, but if we can break it, we'll know for sure. This might be the nail that will seal Capone's coffin for good."

A smile slowly spread on Ness's face as he flipped through the ledger.

Chapter 14

The light from the Chicago Theater sign threw red and white streaks across my apartment. I sat in my armchair, a cigarette glowing between my fingers, a glass of cow's blood slowly congealing on the table. I'd only taken one sip before the vile taste caused me to lose my appetite.

I should have been tired, exhausted even, but my gift prevented that. I was a bit disappointed, because always being awake and alert could sometimes really kill the mood.

It had been a long night at the speakeasy. After Christian had given him the ledger, Ness' entire mood had changed. It was just dumb luck that Christian had recovered it, but Ness didn't care. He'd gone outside to spin a tale to the press—keeping the ledger a secret—but touting the shootout as an escalation of the gang war, and that his team (along with the police) would be soon making the city safe again.

It was all bullshit, but the press lapped it up. When he'd come back in, he hadn't been nice, exactly, but he was cordial and full of praise. At least he'd stopped yelling at us.

Christian and I walked Cloonan and a precinct captain through what had happened. We spun enough lies in order to hide what Brown and I really were that Christian had mumbled something about needing to pray for his sins when we'd finally been able to leave.

Ness was eager to get back to the office to start on the ledger. He was sure that Robsky would be able to eventually crack the code.

I tried to share in the excitement, but it kept eluding me. I was sure now that we'd get Capone for not paying his taxes. It seemed unavoidable at this point, but it left a taste that was more bitter than the cow's blood in my mouth. Sending Capone to jail for not paying taxes, when he'd killed so many people, seemed like a cruel joke.

I picked up the glass of blood, and its rancid odor hit me before it reached my lips.

And now this, I thought. *Is this just a passing thing, or do I have to permanently turn away from cow's blood? What about other animals? Am I now forced to kill people to survive?*

You're not being forced, Saul, Moira said, *it's a choice that you should have made from the beginning. Your body is just reminding you of what I've been telling you all along.*

Just then, there was a knock on my door. *Who the hell...* It was after midnight, so who could be at my door?

I got up and moved quickly to the door. I half expected to feel the tingle of another vampire, somewhat expecting Capone to be on the other side. After tonight, I figured that he'd be angrier than a hornet. But I felt nothing, so it had to be Christian or Ness. (Nobody else from work even knew where I lived.)

I opened the door, prepared to tell Ness or Christian to go away, but froze as I took in the pale, beautiful form of Moira. She wore a sleek, red dress that was set off by a long string of pearls. Her red hair cascaded out from under a wide-brimmed black hat with a red silk band.

She looked lovely, a figure guaranteed to turn a guy's head, but her green eyes were narrow and blazed with a fury that I'd seen before.

"What did I tell you, Saul?"

Her anger radiated off her body. I tried to close the door, but Moira moved even faster than my own enhanced reflexes and, suddenly, her foot was in my apartment, keeping the door open.

I stared at her foot, clearly across the threshold. My own experiences with being unable to enter a person's home told me that this shouldn't be possible.

"You aren't supposed to be in here," I said. It was both a statement of my intent and of my shock. Moira was a vampire, and I had never given her permission to enter *this* apartment. I was confident in my understanding of this effect that my invitation for my previous apartment didn't apply to this one.

"Why not, Saul?" Moira's voice had dropped in pitch, taking on the sharp edge of menace. I had been pushing the door, trying to keep it closed. She shoved it open with what seemed to be a gentle nudge of her arm.

"I don't understand," I spluttered, stepping back from the door. "You're a vampire. You can't come in unless I invite you."

She laughed, and it sounded like ice cubes clinking in a glass—cold, humorless. "Oh, Saul. Did you ever really understand? I'm *so* much more than a vampire now." She held up her left hand, letting the strange bracelet slide down her pale, slender arm. "Nobody tells me what I can and can't do anymore."

Moira took a stroll through my apartment, a slight

85

frown marring her beautiful face as she took in the kitchen, unused bedroom, and living room. She sneered as she spotted the glass of cow's blood.

"It's a shame, Saul. You could have been like Brian, serving at my side." She looked up, but her eyes seemed to be looking at something far away—or long ago. "The humans have a saying, 'blood is thicker than water'. Do you know it?"

It was a rhetorical question, but I found myself nodding. Despite her unexpected appearance here, and the danger and threat that I felt from her, I still wanted to please her.

"It has to do with family, and it can be used by the Blessed as well. A master vampire creates a family. I wanted you to be part of *my* family, but you chose a different path." She casually waved at my apartment, acknowledging it and dismissing it—and me—with a simple gesture.

"Chose? You think I chose to live like this? You did this to me! You and Capone. I never asked for any of this."

"Saul," she said. "Did you get to choose your parents? Your mother and father created your mortal life through their lust. I created your immortal life. I wanted you in *my* family and you rejected me."

I was confused.

Still not unusual, Sarah said.

I ignored my sister. I thought Moira wanted me back. "What's going on, Moira? I thought you'd forgiven me."

"I did, Saul. I told you to follow my rules. I told you not to interfere with me. I told you to stay away." Her voice was rising, becoming more menacing with each word. At some point, her fangs had lengthened. She pointed a finger at me. "But as usual, you just don't listen."

"I thought you loved me, that you wanted us back together."

Moira tilted her head back and laughed. "You were always so gullible, Saul."

You still are, the Moira in my head added.

"You killed me. You drove a fucking chair leg through my heart." Her eyes flashed red and she didn't bother to hide her fangs. "Then you went and became Freed, feeding on a human on your own, creating your own procurator. You were meant to *be mine.*" She punctuated the last words with stabs of her finger. "You belonged to me. I made you, and you took that away. Just like you took Brian away. You were to be part of my family, and instead you chose to destroy it. You will pay for that. Your family will pay for what you've done to me."

Acid filled my stomach as it twisted into a tight knot. "My family? What are you—?" Realization and blood surged through my body, and my fangs grew. "I won't let you hurt my family."

Moira laughed again, and then leapt at me.

Chapter 15

Moira hit me like a ton of bricks. I thought I was ready for it—I mean, we *had* fought before—but the force of the impact surprised me. My knees buckled, and I went down hard as she slashed at me with fingers that had become razor-sharp claws.

That's new! Sarah exclaimed.

Ew, she needs a manicure, Moira added.

I grabbed the pearl necklace and gave a yank. The strand broke—pearls scattered across my floor—but the sudden movement unbalanced her enough for me to throw her off. She rolled away, and I jumped to my feet.

The scratches that she'd given me were already healing, but I couldn't rest. Moira had fought like a maniac the last time, so I knew that I couldn't let up. Not if I was going to save my family.

I rushed forward, prepared to grab Moira and push her against the wall. I needed some kind of advantage and pinning her seemed like the best idea. She crouched, and she met my charge with a punch to my stomach. The blow was so hard that I was lifted off the ground and fell, face first, to the floor, the air in my lungs coming out in a great WHOOSH.

I didn't need the air, but it felt like she'd driven a hammer into my spine. I was stunned for a moment, trying to get back to my feet. I heard a loud SNAP and then a sharp, biting pain in my back. I couldn't turn my head, but my hands could just barely feel the edge of it.

Wood?

I looked to my kitchen and saw one of my chairs shattered, one leg missing.

Ooh… I love the irony, purred the Moira in my head.

I tried to get a grip on the makeshift stake, but my hands were slick with blood. Then a pale ankle in a red heel came into my vision.

"This seems so familiar," Moira said. "But don't worry, love. I don't want you dead. Not yet. I want you alive to see what I am going to do to your family."

"If you hurt them…"

"You'll what? Come after me? Kill me?" She made a *tsk tsk* sound. "Don't you get it, Saul? I *want* you to come after me. I *want* you to see what I will do to your family. I can just picture your expression as you watch your parents get their throats ripped out."

"No!" I tried to get a grip on the chair leg, but a swift kick from Moira knocked my hand away.

"Or maybe I'll let your mother live, and she can serve as my puppet for all eternity."

She crouched before me and lifted my chin with her finger, her claw-like nail digging in, blood dripping from the fresh wound. "Now, your sweet sister, Sarah. She will have a *special* place at my side."

Moira released my chin, and then I felt a blow to the side of my head that was strong enough to—

Chapter 16

I opened my eyes to see a bloody chair leg on the floor before me. I was still on my stomach, but there was no more pain. I reached back and felt a ragged hole in my clothes and tacky blood, but the wound had healed.

I sat up and looked around, but my apartment was empty. Moira's attack was a fresh scar on my mind, and I jumped to my feet. My family was in danger, and I had to get to them. I didn't bother to change, but I grabbed my trench coat to cover my blood-stained clothes as I rushed out the door.

It was still dark, and that gave me an ember of hope that I hadn't been unconscious that long. *Maybe there's still time to save them?*

I broke into a run. I didn't want to wait for the L at this time of night, and hailing a taxi might put the driver at risk. I expected that I would have to face Moira again.

I ran faster than I ever had before, the blocks flying by. I tried to focus on the task at hand, but I couldn't shake the fact that I was going to have to face my parents for the first time since my "death".

I can't wait to see you try to talk your way out of this one, Sarah taunted me.

Leave your brother alone, Mom scolded. *This is serious. How does he tell us that he's been lying to us for over a year?*

Dad added, *Oh, and you think you would have accepted that he's become this monster—*

I'm not a monster, I corrected Dad.

—this vampire if he'd told us? Dad finished, not missing a beat. *You would have made him uncomfortable, insisting that he try to not be a vampire.*

Thanks, Dad.

No. What he needs to worry about is how his boss— that nice Mr. Ness—who has helped him and gave him a job, is going to react. He only had one rule, and now our meshuga *son is going to break that rule.*

To save you!

Feh. How do you know we need saving, eh? Maybe that nafke *was telling a lie? Hmm. Did you even think of that?*

You never even brought her to meet us, like I asked you to do at least a dozen times, Mom added. *How does she even know where we live?*

She could have found it in the city directory, I thought, trying to run faster.

My family fell silent for the last few blocks. The familiar neighborhood was peaceful, which gave me hope that everything was still alright. I opened the door to my parent's building, and flew up the stairs to the second floor.

I paused, trying to sense if anything was wrong. I heard nothing except the snores of neighbors. The only smells that I detected brought back warm memories, as the aromas of onions, cabbage, pierogies, kugel, latkes, and bread emanated from the different apartments, but no blood.

I was relieved, but I hesitated. *Maybe it* was *just a hollow threat?*

When did I ever make a hollow threat? Moira asked,

in my head.

I knocked. The sound was loud in the hallway, and I expected to see familiar faces popping out of neighbor's doors. I knocked again.

Just before I knocked a third time, I heard my father complaining—beseeching God to know who would be disturbing him from a sound sleep and a nice dream. Despite the tension that had tied my stomach into a knot, I smiled a bit.

The lock clicked, and the door opened. My father stood there, his robe on over his pajamas, worn slippers on his feet. His finger was raised in a familiar "I'm going to give you a piece of my mind" gesture.

The tirade didn't come. His jaw went slack, and his eyes widened. "Saul..."

I was desperate to know that Mom and Sarah were safe. I wanted to rush in and search every room, but seeing my father, for the first time in over a year, froze me in place. I could feel my eyes filling with tears.

"No," my father said, pointing his finger at me. "No. What, you tell us a lie for over a year and expect me to be happy to see you? They told us you died. We performed the *tahara* and the *shemira* for you. For seven days we sat *shiva*." He was starting to shake a bit, and I tried to say something, but he cut me off.

"For thirty days we held *shloshim* for you. Your mother was devastated by everything. And now, a year later, you think you can just show up here? Do you expect forgiveness? Do you expect thanks? No." He made a cutting gesture with his hand. "No. From me you get nothing."

"Dad. I can explain. There was a very good reason—"

"Oh, you have a good reason? You think a good reason makes up for all of the grief, and the pain, and the heartache that you put your poor mother through?"

"Can we discuss this inside?" I asked. I was afraid that the neighbors would start poking their heads out, and I still wanted to know that Mom and Sarah were safe.

"Feh." Dad narrowed his eyes and turned away from the door, but he left it open. I took a step to enter, but found the way blocked. I couldn't get my foot over the threshold.

Damnit! Even my own home, where I grew up? How is this fair?

"Dad," I called. "You need to invite me in."

Dad stopped and glared at me. "What? You selfishly lie to us and cause your mother pain, and I should invite you in? Like you're coming over for coffee and to chat? Do you want to talk or are you enjoying hurting us?"

"Dad. Please. Just invite me in. I can explain everything." I shrugged and gestured to the hallway. "I'm fine doing it here in the hallway if you want Mrs. Gershowitz to hear everything." I jerked my thumb over my shoulder toward her door.

"She'll hear everything anyway as soon as she comes over for coffee with your mother. Fine. Saul, my *meshuga* son, please, enter our home."

I ignored the mocking tone and hoped that it would work as an invitation. I took a step forward and let out a breath that I didn't realize that I had held as I walked into my old home. I closed the door and followed Dad, not to the tiny living room, but to the dining room. I sighed inwardly. The dining table was where Dad lectured me and doled out his punishments. He took his place at the head of the table, and I automatically went to my place, feeling like I was ten years old again and getting punished for tipping over Mrs. Gershowitz's geraniums.

"David? What's going on? Who was at the door?" Mom walked into the room and stared at the two of us.

"Go back to bed, Miriam," Dad said.

But Mom didn't hear him. "Saul?" She rushed over and bent down to give me a hug where I sat. "I knew it, Saul. I knew you weren't dead. Through everything, deep down, I knew it couldn't be true."

She broke the hug, and I was about to say something, when she slapped me across the back of my head.

"*That's* for making me suffer for the past year." Another slap. It didn't hurt, but I found myself putting my hands up anyway. "*That's* for making me believe that you were dead."

"Mom! Mom, stop!" I pleaded. I was relieved that both of my parents were okay, and maybe Sarah was, too. *Maybe Moira had been bluffing.*

A bitter *Ha* echoed in my mind. I chose to ignore it.

Mom was still berating me and trying to tell me everything that had happened in the last year at the same time.

"Miriam, please," Dad said, when she paused for a breath. "Saul needs to explain why he lied to us. Why he put us through hell for the past year."

"I didn't mean to do any of that," I protested.

"Oh, so lying about your death and making us suffer was just an accident?"

"You couldn't be bothered to tell us?" Mom started to weep.

"It *was* an accident," I told Dad. Turning to Mom, I added, "and I wanted to tell you the truth, but I was forbidden to see you, or to have any contact with you."

"Forbidden? Who forbade you from telling us? Who

decided that our suffering was a good price for some damn secret?"

"My boss."

"Who is this *paskudnyak?*" Mom asked. "We'll go tell him what a *shmendrik* he's been for making you lie to us."

I held my hands up, happy at how quickly I had steered the blame to Ness, but I needed to know that Sarah was all right.

"Mom, Dad. You can't go to my boss. He doesn't know that I'm here, and I'll lose my job if he ever finds out."

"What kind of boss makes you lie to your parents? That's no boss that I want my son working for."

"I work for the Feds, Dad."

"So? Does your boss care about the emotional trauma that he's caused your poor mother? Feh. Of course not."

"Weren't you working at the Post Office before, dear? Why would you need to lie about your death at the Post Office?"

"Look, I don't have time for this," I said. "I work with Eliot Ness—"

That was a mistake. Both Mom and Dad got all excited by that news. It apparently made up for faking my death.

"Dad," I finally said, getting their attention again. "Some bad people have made threats on you."

"Feh," Dad waved my words aside. "There are lots of bad people around. We can take care of ourselves."

"No, Dad, you can't. Not like this. I can't explain everything—"

"Sure. You want us to believe that we're being threatened, but you can't tell us who is the one doing the threatening."

"Damnit, Dad. Stop it." I was tired of this, and my outburst had stunned them into silence.

"I will explain everything later. But I need to know that Sarah is safe first."

"Sarah? Why wouldn't she be safe?" Dad asked.

"Of course she's safe," Mom said. "She's asleep in her room."

"She didn't run off and fake her death like some people," Dad had to add.

With all of this yelling, why haven't I come out to tell all you schmucks *to be quiet?* Asked the Sarah in my head.

My stomach tied itself into a knot as I got up from the table. I ignored the questions from my parents as I went to Sarah's room. I opened the door and clicked on the light.

My stomach fell to my feet.

Sarah's bed was empty. It had been slept in, but the covers were thrown off.

A gasp came from Mom behind me. "Sarah? Where is she?"

"Was she here last night?" I asked.

"Of course she was here," Dad said, the irritation trying to mask his own fear. "We had dinner and listened to the radio. Your sister worked on her schoolwork. We went to bed."

"She couldn't have gotten out without us knowing about it," Mom said.

I had to force myself to keep my eyes from rolling at that as I stepped up to Sarah's bed. I had snuck out, on more than a few occasions, without getting caught. As I looked at the bed, I saw that a piece of paper had been tucked under Sarah's pillow. I pulled it out. It was a folded piece of plain stationery, with my name written on it in a fine, neat hand.

I hesitated for a moment, and then gingerly opened it up, like it was a bomb about to explode. It only had two lines but, as I read them, my world collapsed.

You took my love from me.
Now I'm taking what you love from you.

Chapter 17

I stared ahead without seeing anything, the edge of my vision tinged with a red haze. The only sound I heard was a dull roar, like the waves of Lake Michigan crashing against the shore. I felt a prick against my lips and tasted blood. My fangs had grown without my realizing that it was happening. It brought me the clarity that I needed, and it allowed me to focus back on Sarah's room.

Mom was crying. Dad was calling my name. I continued to face Sarah's bed, and I looked down to see that Moira's note had been crumpled into a ball in my hands. I wanted to be angry. I wanted to race out of the house to find Moira. To find Sarah.

But I couldn't do that. I needed to be strong for my parents. I shoved my anger down, pushing it into a corner where it could sit and simmer. I'd use it soon enough.

I composed myself and took a calming breath. I didn't need the air, but it was a good illusion for my parents, plus, the physical action of taking the breath allowed me to retract my fangs and compose my face. Even though my parents thought I hadn't died—at least from their perspective—I wasn't ready to reveal everything to them. That sort of shock wouldn't be good for them, and I didn't want to deal with the questions that knowledge would bring.

"Saul, where is she? Do you know where Sarah is?"

Dad's voice sounded tired. I turned to see him holding my mother as she sobbed into his shoulder. He looked much older than I'd ever seen him before.

"I don't know," I said, anguish eating at my heart as I saw Dad's face fall. "But I will find out. I work for the Feds now. For Eliot Ness. I have access to resources. I *will* find Sarah."

This lifted Dad's spirits, and it wasn't a lie, but I wasn't going to involve Ness. Not at first. But I would find Sarah.

Dad took Mom back to their room. I headed to the door, but he called out to me before I could leave. I stopped and waited for him. "Find your sister, Saul." He pointed his finger at me, imploring me to do something. "You *do* this. You need to bring Sarah home to us. Safe."

"I plan on it," I said. I gave him a reassuring smile, and he grabbed me and gave me a fierce hug. "Bring your sister home. If you don't, I don't know what will happen with your mother."

I hugged him back and whispered, "I will."

We broke our embrace, and I left. Once I was outside the building, I broke into a run.

I am going to find you, Moira. I will find you and get Sarah back.

Then what, love? It was the voice of the new Moira this time, rather than my phantom Moira.

I will destroy you.

Big talk, tough guy. How will you do that? I handled you pretty easily earlier tonight.

I shook my head, waving the phantom away like an annoying insect. I put my energy into running. I was feeling the effort as I skidded to a stop in front of Pandora's Legacy. The poolroom was locked up, but I wasn't going to let that stop me.

As I reached for the door, prepared to rip it open, a voice came from the dark alley behind me. It was scratchy and rough.

"You won't find her there."

I turned. I'd been so focused on getting here that I hadn't checked the area first. A faint glimmer of light touched the eastern horizon, but it was still as dark as midnight in the alley. It didn't matter to me, and I spotted the man who had spoken sitting next to several trash bins. It was a vagrant, but his words told me that he was more than just a simple bum.

He didn't seem to be surprised when I appeared out of thin air in front of him. "Where is she?" I growled.

"She left. She said you'd come here, though. She said to tell you that if you come after her, she won't stop with your sister. She'll take your parents, too."

I tapped into the anger that I'd hidden away in the dark corner. My fangs jutted out as I grabbed the stinking bum, lifting him to his feet. "Where is Moira?"

"She's not here," the bum said again, giving me a contemptuous smile. He wasn't afraid of me even as I tightened my grip and lifted him off the ground. "You won't find her. Give up, Saul. Your sister now belongs to my master. You will never get—"

"No!" He never finished his thought as I bit into his throat, the words merely a gurgle as I ripped into him. Blood sprayed from his neck as I tore away his flesh. Then I was feeding, draining the blood from him. In only a few seconds, I was done, his lifeless body limp in my hands.

Damnit! I did it again!

Mmm.. Moira moaned. *It feels glorious, doesn't it?*

No, I lied.

Now, Saul, Moira scolded, *you know you can't lie to me. You'd just be lying to yourself.*

I couldn't stop.

You didn't want to stop. You knew what would happen. You knew how good it would feel, how much better it would be than that awful cow's blood.

That doesn't make it right.

Right? You are one of the Blessed. Whatever we do, that's what's 'right.' Who's going to stop us?

Me.

Disgusted with myself, I threw the corpse far back into the dark alley. I swept the back of my hand across my mouth, cleaning the small traces of blood away. I straightened my coat and headed up the street toward Logan's Square.

Chapter 18

The taxi pulled up outside of Christian's apartment building. I paid the driver and stood on the sidewalk as the cab pulled away. After a moment, I walked inside and took the stairs up to his floor. It was still early in the morning, but I knew from the smell of toast and coffee that Christian was already awake.

I knocked and waited a moment before the door opened. Unlike other times, where he'd "greeted" me with crosses and holy water, Christian's reaction at seeing me was to sigh loudly, but then his eyes widened. He held the door wide and ushered me inside.

"Mary and Joseph, what happened to you? Are you alright?" He closed the door as I looked down and saw the bloodstains on my shirt. Some were old and dried, but others still had the red sheen and glimmer of fresh blood.

Christian walked into his small kitchen. "No, I'm fine," I reassured him.

He stopped and gave me his preacher look, the one that he used when he was sure that I'd done something monstrous and I should confess my sins. It didn't work, since I was Jewish, and I knew better than to tell Christian the truth, especially about this. I *had* done something monstrous—he'd definitely see it that way—and I needed his help to save Sarah. If he knew what I'd just done to Moira's messenger, he'd probably stick a stake through my heart, despite our special relationship, and I wouldn't blame him.

"Moira came to my apartment last night," I said, instead. This caused Christian's eyebrows to crawl up his forehead. He went over to a cabinet and pulled out a coffee mug.

"She was mad that I had interfered with her plans. Mad that I had killed Mr. Brown."

Christian poured coffee into the mug and set it before me. I ignored the cup. "Did you...?" He didn't finish the sentence, but I knew what he meant.

"No." I put my hands around the mug and stared at its contents. "She was... a monster." I looked up. "She wasn't stopped by my threshold. And she was stronger. Faster. She laid me out with a single blow. Then she pinned me to the floor with a chair leg."

Christian's eyes widened as he caught the irony of the situation. "But how did...?"

"She wanted me alive. She knocked me out and, when I came to, the chair leg had been removed."

"Why did she do that? Was she just giving you a warning?"

I finally picked up the coffee and took a drink, trying to organize my thoughts. "She was really mad, but she doesn't want me dead. She wants me to suffer. She took her."

"Took who?"

"My sister. Sarah."

Christian's eyes went wide, and he quickly made the sign of the cross.

"She said that since I took her love from her—"

"Mr. Brown." I nodded.

"That she'd take something I loved. I raced to my parents place—"

"Your parents know you didn't die?"

I ignored his accusatory tone and nodded. "By the time I got there, Sarah was already gone. Moira has her." The sadness I'd been feeling as I recounted the events turned to bitter acid. I had to set the mug down before it broke in my hands.

"Moira is something... else," I said. "She's no longer just a vampire. I don't know what she is, but I'm going to stop her. I'm going to save Sarah."

"But how?"

Leave it to Christian to throw cold water on things. But this time, I had an answer for him. "I'm going to get help."

"Help? From whom?"

"A friend." Christian gave me a dubious look. "He's the one who told me about the vampire war last year, before we went to Atlantic City. He went to Kansas City, and he's the only one that can help me."

Christian nodded, but asked, "How can he help?"

"He's a vampire, but he's not like Capone, Mr. Brown, or me."

Christian folded his arms and leaned against the counter. "Not like you? He's a vampire, how is he not like you?"

I hesitated. "I don't know. He's different somehow." I thought back to our brief encounter on the rooftop that overlooks my parent's apartment. The image of Joe's contorted face, full of anger and rage, came to mind. "He's more... wild. Feral."

"A feral vampire?"

"And I can't sense him, and some other things."

Christian gave me a look and uncrossed his arms. "A vampire is a vampire; your kind don't come in different varieties like apples."

"Look, I don't know how to explain it any better. He's different, and he's the only one who can possibly help me. If I can convince him to come to Chicago, we can save Sarah."

"Didn't you tell me last year that he didn't want to get involved? Why would he be willing to help now?"

"I just know he will. We were friends. He knew about Sarah. He'll agree to help me."

Christian looked down at his own coffee for a moment, and then looked up. "Fine. When do we leave?"

I shook my head. "*I'll* leave later today, but I want you to stay here. We need to find Moira."

"Isn't she at the pool hall?"

"No. I already looked." It was mostly the truth. The image of me ripping out the messenger's throat flashed in my head. I couldn't tell Christian the whole truth.

That's because he'd stake you if he knew, Moira said.

He only did what he had to do, Mom chided her. *He's a good boy.*

Oh, I agree, Moira added. *He finally did what he should have been doing from the beginning.*

That's not what she meant, and you know it, Sarah retorted.

Feh! Dad snorted. *Why any of you listen to this* nafka, *I'll never know.*

I mean, cow's blood? Moira continued, unfazed. *Just the thought of it makes me shudder.*

It's not that bad, I countered. *Once you get used to it.*

Get used to it?! Moira practically screamed. *You are one of the Blessed. You don't need to sully yourself by standing in line to eat day-old bread when you can feast like a king on an endless buffet whenever you desire. You have the power, Saul. The only one that's stopping you is you.*

And I couldn't even do that *right,* I sighed.

Christian paused and drank his coffee. When he put the cup down, he looked me in the eyes—something he rarely did—and said, "Have you considered that you might not be able to save your sister?"

"No." I spat out the word, hoping to keep the bitter taste of failure out. "No," I said again, more calmly. "Moira wants me to suffer, to make me pay for interfering with her plans. She could have killed my parents, but she didn't, even though she told me that she would. I have to believe that she won't kill Sarah."

"What if Moira doesn't want to *just* kill her?"

"What?"

"We—you—killed Mr. Brown. He was her right-hand man. She may want to rebuild her power. What if she wants to replace Brown with Sarah?"

I didn't think that I could feel cold as a vampire, but a chill ran along my spine. *Moira was making a family.*

And you know how important family is, Moira said.

So that's *why you wanted me?* I asked.

We could have done so much together. You were supposed to be by my side, but you just couldn't play along, could you? You just couldn't accept the gift I gave you.

Gift? More like a curse.

Maybe you can exchange it for a nice pair of socks, Sarah quipped.

Enough! Moira spat. *You don't want to join me, and you've killed Brian, so now you're going to suffer the consequences.*

"All the more reason to get help," I said.

Christian nodded. "I will try to find Moira. And I will try to keep Ness happy about you being gone."

I had completely forgotten about Ness, Capone, and everything else. None of that mattered to me now. I nodded my thanks and stood up.

"Find Sarah," I said, as I walked to the door. "I can't save her without your help."

Chapter 19

I returned to my apartment and ignored the mess and all the blood that was staining the floor. My blood. I stepped over the bloodstains, knocking some pearls aside as they rolled under my side table. I changed, grabbed a few items, and left as fast as I could. I thought about grabbing a thermos of blood, but just the idea of it made my stomach churn, so I left it behind. I took a taxi to Union Station, and I was able to get a ticket for the westbound train before it left that morning.

I don't remember the journey. I looked out of the window for the entire trip, but the countryside passed by in an unfocused blur. My mind was a jumbled mess as I repeatedly thought about what Moira might be doing to Sarah, then tried to convince myself that she'd be alright. Every time that I calmed myself down, I would think of some new, cruel way that Moira could hurt Sarah, and the cycle would begin again.

Sometime after noon, I forced myself up and headed to the club car. I paid a nickel for a Coke and sat at a table. We were—somewhere. Iowa? Missouri? It was all farms, and they all looked the same to me. (Look—I grew up in the city, and the only reason that I know that beef comes from a cow is because Dad works at the stockyards.)

I turned away from the window and pulled out a postcard from my coat. It was a drawing of a tall brick building, looking at it from one corner, as if you stood across the street and could see up the two streets on either side. At the bottom was printed "Hotel Muehlebach. Kansas City, Missouri."

I turned the card over and, under the postcard's text declaring, "Three famous dining rooms," was scrawled a short message.

Finally settled in and found a good job here slinging hash. If you want to give up all that stress there, come join me. I can get you hired on. Joe.

I'd gotten the card back in September of last year. I'd laughed at the thought of Joe working as a cook, and then I'd tossed the card into a drawer. I'd grabbed it this morning as I left my apartment.

There was no return address, but I was pretty sure that Joe had specifically sent me this card to tell me where he was working. I hoped that he was still working there now, six months later.

I finished the Coke, twirling the postcard between my fingers as I ran through what I would say to Joe. Despite what I'd told Christian, I had no assurance that Joe would return with me to Chicago. When he'd left last year, he'd been very adamant that he would not get involved. My only hope was to get him to agree that saving Sarah was worth him returning, and that was a far stretch as well. I'd told Christian that Joe would do this for her, but despite us working together, Joe had never met my sister, and he only knew that I had one because I talked a lot during our work shifts.

Joe had been my best (only) friend at the Post Office, but it turned out that I barely knew the guy. I only knew what he'd told me, which hadn't been a lot, and didn't include the fact that he was a vampire. When I asked him to take on Capone, he had shouted his anger, but I also got the feeling that there was more going on. Regret, sadness, and maybe fear. I had to hope that I could leverage those feelings so that he could help keep Sarah from turning into something like me.

The train arrived at Kansas City's Union Station just before five pm. As I left the station, I could see a spire of concrete rising from a hill south of the station. I hailed a cab and told the driver to take me to the Muehlebach Hotel.

"Sure thing, bub." We drove off and, in about five minutes, he let me out in front of the hotel's entrance.

The inside of the hotel was dark wood, polished brass, and white and black tile. My first thought was to go to reception and see if anybody there knew Joe, but then I heard the sound of laughter, the clink of glass, and picked out the smells of cigars mixed with beef and potatoes. I turned that way, figuring that the best way to find Joe was to try one of the "three famous dining rooms."

I walked down some steps, opened a door that was inlaid with a distinctive green-and-orange stained glass window, and stepped down into a small room. It was a smoking lounge, not a dining room, but people here had drinks and food, so I continued over to the bar.

"What can I get you, mister?" asked a man who was a bit younger than Dad.

"I'm looking for Joe Klein. You know him?"

The man's forehead crinkled up. "If he owes you any money or anything, then he's not here."

"Nothing like that," I said with a smile. "Tell him a friend from Chicago is here to say hi."

The man gave me a long look, and then walked through

a door—to the kitchen, I assumed. I was surprised that I'd hit pay dirt the first time. I pulled out one of my Chesterfields and lit it. I'd barely had a chance to enjoy it before I heard, "Saul!" coming from the door.

A few of the room's patrons looked up at the same time I did. Joe stood in the doorway, a greasy apron tied around his waist. He walked around the bar to me. I stuck out my hand, but he gave me a hug instead. I could hear a couple of quiet snickers from the other side of the room, but I patted him on the back.

Joe broke our embrace and took off his apron. "Paul, I'm going to take my break now."

He said it casually, but I could feel the command that echoed below the words. Paul took the apron and said, "Sure thing, Joe." I wondered how many times Joe had done that when we worked at the Post Office, and why he'd apparently never done it with Francine.

Joe gestured to the doors, and we walked up the steps and headed outside.

Chapter 20

Joe pulled out his cigarettes. I caught the distinctive red package of his Morleys as we walked out the doors. The sun was beginning to touch the horizon. Joe let out a puff of smoke. "It's been a while, Saul. How's it going?"

I wanted to blurt everything out, to tell him what had happened with Capone, Christian, Moira and Mr. Brown, and Sarah. The words begged to spill from my lips, but I was afraid that, if I spilled my guts, I would drive Joe away and ruin any chance at getting his help.

"Things are good," I lied. There was the slightest of pauses as he placed the cigarette to his lips, but he didn't call me out on the lie.

"So, have you come to your senses?" He asked, blowing out more smoke. "I think I can get you a decent job as a cook if you're ready to leave all the glitz and glam in Chicago." He looked at me, narrowing his eyes. "You *do* know how to cook, don't you?"

"I'm a bit rusty. I haven't cooked a meal in over a year."

Joe shook his head. "Yeah, it's probably not a good idea to have you poison the guests. Maybe we can start you out as a waiter." He pointed at me with the cigarette. "But you should cook stuff. It's a good skill to learn and it keeps your neighbors from asking questions because they never catch the smell of food coming from your apartment."

I nodded at the advice, since it made sense, but longed

for more of it. This was the kind of information that I was missing by not having a mentor—somebody who could show me the ropes. "I didn't know you could cook," I said. We'd always eaten at the coffee shop in the Post Office building, and we never talked about domestic activities when we'd sorted the mail.

Joe finished his cigarette and dropped it to the sidewalk, crushing it with his heel. "There's a lot about me that you don't know." He checked for traffic, and then jogged across the street. I followed.

"So, what's the scoop? You didn't come here for a job, and I doubt that you came all this way to just flap your gums."

"I need your help."

Joe's step paused briefly, but then continued. He stayed silent.

"Moira's back."

The silence reigned as we crossed another street, then Joe said, "That dame you were dating. Didn't you say that she went missing last year? Isn't that good? Your girl is back. Why do you sound like this is a bad thing?"

"She's a vampire."

Joe whistled, but kept his mouth shut, so I continued, "She's the one who made me—I guess. I'm a bit fuzzy on how all that works."

Joe stopped walking, and shook his head. "You know, I thought there was something dangerous about her when you two first met."

"You could sense that she was a vampire?"

"Oh, hell, no. But any dame who was interested in you had to be dangerous." He grinned, and I slugged him in the shoulder. His arm was like stone, but he put up his hand to pretend like I'd hurt him."

"But I did wonder. Especially after you said that she went missing, when you started acting all weird."

"I didn't act weird," I protested.

"Uh huh. Sneaking around the building at night. Searching the city for this dame. Clandestine meetings with the Feds."

I think my mouth opened a little, and Joe tapped his ear. "Vampire senses, remember? Besides, you really weren't all that careful."

I had to nod my head at that. The parade of gangsters, Feds, and monsters through my apartment attested to just how crazy my life had been at that time.

Yes, your life is definitely back to normal now, Sarah teased.

"What's happened to you, Saul? This isn't just about your maker coming back. Things have changed. I can tell you are no longer a Vegan."

"How can you tell I'm no longer a Vegan?"

Joe tapped his nose. "Vampire senses, remember? You smell different."

"I don't smell."

"*You* don't, but it's something that I can sense. I'm sure a fancy scientist could explain it." He started walking again. "What else has happened?"

So, I broke down and finally started telling my tale in earnest. I told him about working with Ness to stop Capone. I told him about being partnered with Christian and what I knew of the Night Watchers. I told him about my feeding on Christian and my fight with Brian on the boardwalk in Atlantic City. I told him about Capone getting arrested and then getting out of jail. I sheepishly told him about killing the owner of Pandora's Legacy. Then I told him about Moira's return and killing Brian. At that, his eyes widened in surprise, but he made no comment. Through it all, he was silent, nodding his head several times, and lighting and smoking three cigarettes while he listened to my rambling.

"But Moira's changed. She's different. She attacked me the other night, and she was stronger, faster. Way stronger than Brian had been. Stronger than when I fought her the first time, before I had even become a vampire."

Joe stopped, and I noticed that we'd walked all the way to a hill south of Union Station that had a tall concrete tower on it. A pair of sphinxes and two large buildings—they looked like mausoleums—flanked the tower.

"Just leave Chicago, Saul. It's obvious that you can't stop Moira, so just leave. Come to Kansas City. You can stay with me. My apartment isn't that big, but we don't really need to sleep, do we? Nobody in Chicago will miss you."

He just didn't understand. I hadn't told him the worst part yet. "I can't leave. I *won't* leave. Moira took my sister. She took Sarah and I need to get her back. I have to save her. I have to protect her, so that she doesn't die. Or even worse, becomes like me."

The words had tumbled out nearly in a single breath, but I thought that my words may have had the effect that I wanted. Joe was slowly nodding his head as he looked up at the tower.

"Please, Joe. You're the only one who can help me save my sister."

Joe lowered his gaze and looked me in the eyes. "No."

Chapter 21

The single syllable was a punch to my gut. Before I knew it, my hand was flying to Joe's head. He neatly side-stepped my punch, but I didn't care.

Well, I guess it's curtains for me, Sarah sighed.

"You have to help me! You're the only one who can! I have to save Sarah!" I threw more punches, but none of them connected as Joe danced around them better than Jack Dempsey. Then he grabbed my arm, and he twisted it around my back. In a blur—even to my eyes—he stood behind me.

"Take it easy, Saul. Let me explain."

Oh, this should be good. I can't wait to hear you explain why you want to just let me die, Sarah commented, anger seeping in more and more with each word.

I didn't want to hear any explanation. Tears were running down my face. My anger had melted into sadness and fear. "I don't know anybody else. You are my only hope. You're my last chance to save Sarah."

"Are you finished throwing your tantrum? Can I let you go now?"

I nodded, and Joe let go of my arm. I took a couple of steps, and then turned to face him.

"I'm sorry, Saul. I made a vow, a very long time ago, that I would never get involved with other vampires again."

"But if you don't help me, my sister will die."

Joe gave an almost imperceptible shrug of his shoulders, and I nearly lost it again.

Some friend he's turned out to be, Sarah mocked.

Oh, I'm looking forward to what I'm going to do to her, Moira's voice purred.

I gritted my teeth and had to force my fangs from coming out. I didn't need this distraction. I had to get Joe to change his mind.

"So that's it. You really don't care. You're fine with condemning my sister to death—or worse." I didn't keep the bitterness from my voice.

"I do care." His words were quiet, almost a whisper that even I had to strain to hear. "But I won't—I *can't*—get involved. Not again."

Joe turned his back and looked up at the tower. Floodlights had come on, and they bathed the building in a harsh, white light. He turned back to me and pulled out his pack of smokes.

"Damnit, I don't have time for this." I turned to head down the hill, back to the station.

"Saul."

I ignored Joe and continued walking.

"Saul, wait." I felt a rush of air and, suddenly, Joe stood in front of me. I tried to go around him, but he kept dancing in front of me to block my way.

"Damnit, Joe! If you won't help me, then get out of my fucking way! I'm going to save my sister, even if it kills me."

"Saul, I have my reasons for not going back to Chicago. I won't get directly involved again."

I waved my hand to shoo him away. I was done with this. But he held up his hand, a cigarette held between his fingers.

"But I might be able to help you."

I paused, my hope sparking back to life. "How?"

"Did you ever wonder why you could never 'feel' me? How I was able to spy on you when you went to watch your parents? Or why I didn't know that Moira was a vampire?"

I shrugged, "Sure, but how does that help me save Sarah?"

"I'm getting to that." Joe took a drag on his Morley and walked back up toward the top of the hill. I followed him with a sigh.

"Did you know that there are two kinds of vampires?" He gave me a look.

"I knew it! Christian wouldn't believe me when I tried to explain it to him, but I knew there had to be something. So, are we like different races or something?"

"If you want to think of it like that. There are vampires like you and Capone—"

"Yeah, Moira called us 'Blessed'. Capone said we were the 'Enlightened'."

Joe laughed. "I bet he did." He took a pull from the cigarette. "There are vampires like you. Your kind comes from one… I guess, bloodline, is the best term for it. Then there are vampires like me. I come from another bloodline, descended from the first vampires. My kind call us the pure line."

"Really? And you laugh at what Capone calls himself?" I gave a derisive chuckle. "And so, I'm what? Impure?"

"I really don't like to use the terms myself, but the insulting term others like me use for your kind is 'leeches'."

I shook my head. "That's original."

"Look," Joe dropped the cigarette and crushed it under his shoe. "None of that matters. Not to me, at least. It's just important to know that there are two types."

"Fine. So, there are two types of vampires. So what?"

"We all share similar abilities. We have all of the same strengths and weaknesses."

"Yeah—about those. What are they? What can I do? I mean, I know some stuff, but there's a lot I don't know."

"Do you want to stay and find out?" Joe asked. "I can't really explain it all in a short time. Certainly not in a few minutes."

Damnit! How will I ever learn everything I can do? I can't take the time to find out. I need to save Sarah.

Big brother to the rescue. How sweet, Moira joked.

"I don't have the time to stay," I said. "I need to head back to Chicago tonight. So, how can you help me if the two types of vampires are the same?"

"I said we share the same abilities, but we are not the same. My kind is stronger. You know how different you felt when you went from being a Vegan to a full vampire?"

"Yeah." I felt my cheeks flush from embarrassment.

"Well, imagine that same type of change, but for me compared to you."

I'll admit, my eyes widened at that. "You can do that—for me, I mean?"

Joe gave a reluctant nod. "I think so. But there are risks with this. Things you should consider."

My mind raced. *I can be stronger than Moira and Capone. I can save Sarah.*

And that's what really matters here, Sarah added.

"I don't care," I said. "If I can save my sister, I don't care what the risks are."

"Are you sure? I think you should at least know what—"

"No." I cut him off with a slash of my hand. "Whatever the risks are, I'll take them so I can save Sarah."

"No, Saul. You have to understand. I have done horrible, unspeakable things since I became a vampire."

"You said that in Chicago." I felt my stomach tighten just a bit. "What things?"

"I won't talk about them now. Remember you said that you were afraid of becoming like Capone? Becoming a monster?"

"Well, that didn't last," I scoffed. "I turned into a monster anyway."

Joe shook his head. "If I do this, you will be much more of a monster than you are now."

Images of Moira attacking me, visions of her taking Sarah, and of her attacking my parents flashed through my head like rapid-fire photographs, flashbulbs exploding as each new, and more horrible, image hit me. "I don't care. Whatever it takes. Whatever the risks. *I will save Sarah.*"

Joe gave a subtle shrug, and then nodded.

"What do I do?"

"We feed on each other. I feed on you and then you need to feed on me."

"That's it?" It seemed too easy to be true.

"That's it," Joe confirmed.

I looked around. It was getting late, but there were still a few people strolling through the area to take in the spire of concrete. "Do we do it here, or someplace else?"

"We can do it here," Joe said with an impish smile. "Nobody will notice us."

"Okay." I pulled up my sleeve and Joe gave me a look. "What?"

"I'm used to the more traditional method." He tapped the side of his neck. "But if you prefer the wrist, that's fine. It doesn't really matter where we do it."

I hesitated, but continued to pull up my sleeve. Joe took

my arm and bit into it. There was only a minor pricking sensation. Almost instantaneously, there was then no feeling at all, like my wrist had gone numb. My only other experience of being bitten by a vampire had been with Moira, and this felt nothing like that. Granted, at the time, I'd been too distracted by our lovemaking to remember that she had actually even bitten me.

You were delicious, Moira's voice purred.

I watched Joe drink my blood, his lips pressed to my skin, his throat moving as he swallowed. And then he was finished, barely a minute after he'd started. He lifted his head and, other than a reddish hue to his lips, he didn't look any different.

"Your turn." He held out his wrist. I lifted it to my mouth, my fangs already extended, and I bit into his wrist.

I heard Christian's voice in my head, *Feed on me.* His face, the carousel, and the smell of popcorn filled my senses. Then I tasted Joe's blood. It was rich, thick. I imagined it being the blood of all the vampires before him, an unending history of pure-blooded vampires going back to the dawn of mankind. I could feel my heart racing. *Was this due to the blood, or just my own excitement?*

I stopped after a minute, just like Joe had done. I let go of his wrist and he gave me a reassuring smile. "Feel any different?" he asked.

"I don't know."

"Give it time. I still think you should stay here, but I know you won't." He stuck out his hand. "Good luck." I shook his hand. "I hope you can save your sister. I really do. Nobody deserves to become what we have become."

Chapter 22

The club car was mostly empty as the train headed across... Iowa? Illinois? I don't know, it was night and, even with my enhanced vision, all I saw were farms and farmhouses, their occupants all tucked safely into their beds.

Sometime after the train left Kansas City, I started feeling... different. My senses had been sharper since I'd fed on Craig at the pool hall, but I soon realized that they were now even more enhanced. It was hard to gauge just how much better they were while I was on the train, but I could tell that there was a difference.

I also realized that I was stronger. I had been sitting and fantasizing about all the things I had wanted to do to Moira when I had accidentally broken the Coke bottle that I'd been holding. It had just shattered in my hand, the Coke spilling everywhere. The attendant had apologized about that, even though I was the one who'd made the mess, and he had given me a replacement Coke for free.

That's when I noticed another difference. I was *aware* of the attendant. I knew where he was as he moved about, even when I wasn't watching him. It wasn't like the tingling sensation that I got with vampires. This was just a subtle *knowing* in my subconscious. As I thought more about it, I could identify the other people in the club car as well. A man who smoked Morleys wore too much aftershave. A woman who was nursing a seltzer water used a lavender-scented shampoo. She was with a man who was nervous, sweating, and laughing too much. All of this rushed me at once, in a barrage of sounds and smells. I mean, before, I'd been able to tell what someone like Cloonan or Friel had had for lunch, but I'd had to concentrate on the act of smelling. Now, it all just came to me.

The scary thing to me was that I also knew that the man with the Morleys was sick. He was ill with something. I don't know what kind of illness: polio, TB, just a common cold? But I *knew* that he was sick.

A memory came to me, then, of Mom, Dad, Sarah, and me visiting the Lincoln Park Zoo. I remembered the Lion House and, in the exhibit, it said that lions would target the sick and the weak when they hunted. I realized then that these new senses were better because I was now a hunter. A predator. The man who was chain-smoking his Morleys? He was my prey.

That's also when I realized that it had been nearly twenty-four hours since I had last fed. Everyone in the club car smelled like food. I could smell their blood and feel their hearts beating. My fangs itched with anticipation, wanting, begging to be extended.

I rushed out of the club car, standing on the small platform between cars. The fresh air helped remove some of the odor, and I quickly lit a smoke to mask the rest of it. The feeling passed, and I stayed out on the platform for a long time, at least until the other passengers finally left the car so that I felt comfortable returning.

As the trip progressed, I continued to stare out the window, drinking my fifth Coke and smoking my—I counted the butts in the ashtray—nineteenth cigarette. (I'd already had to buy a new pack.) The cigarettes helped to mask the smell of the club car attendant, who was reading a *Weird Tales* magazine and trying not to look too bored. The thought struck me, then, that Joe smoked like a chimney, and I wondered if he did it for the same reason: to mask the smell of our prey.

I shook my head, swirled the Coke in its bottle, and thought about Christian in order to take my mind off of how *good* the attendant smelled. If I kept thinking about the attendant, he'd end up dead and I would become a murderer.

Again, Sarah said.

Shut up!

I hoped that Christian had been successful in finding out where Moira had taken Sarah. Now that I had new powers, I wanted to use them. I wanted to make Moira pay. She'd surprised me before (on two occasions) but, this time, I had a surprise of my own.

The sun rose, and soon we were entering the outskirts of Chicago. I was relieved when the train pulled into Union Station. I left the car and headed to the main concourse. That was a terrible mistake.

It was like walking into the stockyards. Everywhere, all around me, I smelled blood. *Food.* People—*prey*—walked past me and all around the large space.

How does Joe handle this? In no way will a cigarette mask this *scent.* I raced outside. I needed to get away from all of the people, but the craving was too strong. It had now been over a full day since I'd fed, and my body screamed for nourishment.

I spied a businessman walking down the sidewalk and picked him, like I was an African lion hunting a gazelle. I started to follow him.

What in the hell am I doing?

What our kind has been doing for a long time, love. Moira's voice urged me on.

The man crossed the road, and I continued after him.

No! I am not a monster!

Moira's laugh filled my head. *Oh, it's much too late for that, darling.*

Why are you doing this, Saul? Dad's voice said. *This nafka did this to you. She took our Sarah, and you still let her into your head? Forgive him Lord, for he is an imbecile and knows not what he's doing.*

It's because you still love me. Right, Saul? Moira laughed again. *I will always be a part of you. Forever.*

I stopped and gripped a light post. *No. Dad's right. I can't kill you if you're still in my head.* The man was walking away. I wanted to follow him. My body yearned to run up to him and drink his blood, but I forced myself to turn and run up an alley.

You couldn't control me before, I told the Moira in my head. *And I won't let you control me now.*

That's cute, Saul, but, again, you're just lying to yourself. I am you. You can't run away from yourself.

I saw another person, a middle-aged woman carrying a basket with groceries, and the urge to feed hit me again. It was even stronger than before. I focused on the woman as she walked. I could strike so fast that she wouldn't know what had happened.

You're weak, Saul. You'll never be able to kill me. Now, let's feed!

I focused on my target, and suddenly found myself running. I was moving so fast that they wouldn't see me. And then, I was past the sidewalk and down the alley. I reached out and grabbed my prey.

The woman continued walking, oblivious to my presence in the shadows of the alley. As I bit into the rat, its blood tasted foul, like burnt meat, but I didn't gag or throw up. In seconds, I had drained all of the rat's blood. I tossed the dead rat to the ground.

I was still hungry, but the immediate urge to feed was gone. And the best thing of all? Moira had finally shut up.

Chapter 23

I returned to my apartment. I needed to find Christian, but I also needed a change of clothes and a shower. I also really wanted to brush my teeth. The rat had curbed my craving, but it disgusted me when I thought about drinking its blood.

My apartment was still a mess when I returned, and I found a note that had been slipped under my door. It was from the landlord, threatening to kick me out if there were any more disturbances. I'd have to pay him a visit in order to "straighten" things out.

I opened the refrigerator and got out some cow's blood to warm while I got cleaned up. After a shower and a change of clothes, I ignored the rest of the mess and headed into the kitchen, where I poured a glass of blood. It still smelled wrong to me, but it wasn't repulsive. I took a drink and… didn't gag. It didn't taste all that great, like meat that was slightly off, but I could drink it without issue.

Is this another benefit of Joe's blood?

Nobody answered me. It was yet another question that I would probably never get the answer to. I finished the glass, and I was now ready to find Christian. It was Friday, so it was possible that Christian was already at work but, since I'd asked him to find Sarah, I was hoping that he'd not gone in today. I decided that the simplest thing to do was to go to his apartment. If he wasn't there, I would then go into work and try to avoid Ness's wrath.

Thankfully, I didn't have to face Ness, as Christian was at home. He let me in.

"Where's your friend?"

"He's not coming," I said, as I went into Christian's living room.

"He won't help you?" I heard a bit of sadness in his voice, and I smiled at knowing that Christian *did* care about Sarah.

"I didn't say that. He gave me some of his power, so I can take on Moira now."

"His power? How does that help? I told you there are not different types of vampires. You couldn't stop Moira before, so how does having his 'power' help you?"

"That's where you're wrong," I smiled, happy with the thought that I knew something that the Night Watchers didn't.

"I've been an agent in the Night Watchers for over ten years. I think I would know if there were different vampire types out there."

"Care to bet on that?" I said, and when Christian remained quiet, I chuckled. "There are different types, different bloodlines. My friend is a pure vampire." That elicited a snort from Christian. "While Capone, Moira, and me are of a different bloodline."

"Let me guess, impure?"

I waved his sarcasm away. "He gave me his power, so I know there is a difference. I feel different. I'm stronger and faster than I was before and my senses are better."

Christian shrugged, clearly unimpressed with what I had become. "How did your friend give you this power?"

"We had to feed on each other."

Christian made the sign of the cross and shook his head.

He went and sat down in his armchair by the radio. I sat down in the other chair.

"What about you? Did you find out where Moira is hiding? Where she took Sarah?"

As soon as Christian reached for the cross around his neck, I knew the answer.

"I tried," he started. I didn't let him get any more out.

"You had one fucking job!" My anger boiled over. Suddenly I was standing, looming over Christian. "How can you not have found them?"

I continued yelling, I think. Christian was sitting back in the chair, eyes wide. I'd felt my fangs enlarge, and my face screwed up into a mask of anger.

Christian ripped the silver crucifix from his neck and thrust it at me. I don't know why; I'd never before been repelled by the sight of the cross. Then I felt a burning on my cheek. My anger was washed away by the flash of hot pain. I took a step back and sat down.

"What the hell?" I gingerly touched my cheek and felt a cross-shaped scar. "That hurt."

"Do not threaten me again, spawn of Satan." Christian's hand was shaking, and I could see curls of smoke coming from the crucifix. He'd slipped into his evangelical mode. "I choose to help you but, if you do that again, I will rid the Earth of your unholy existence."

"Why did that hurt, though?"

Christian shrugged. "It is a blessed symbol of my faith. Just like the holy water. Clearly it hurts because of the evil within you."

"You know I'm not evil," I said. But by the look that Christian gave me, he was thinking of the man that I'd killed at the pool hall. It was a good thing that he didn't know about the bum that I'd killed outside the pool hall, or he'd likely nail that cross to my head.

I touched my cheek again. The scar was already healing, but the pain lingered. "I'm sorry," I said.

Christian relaxed, but he kept the cross in his hand. "I looked everywhere for Moira," he finally said. "I pulled in a few contacts and called in some favors. Nobody knows anything."

"Are they lying?"

He shrugged. "Maybe. But I got the feeling that nobody knew who she was. Maybe she's bewitched them into forgetting her, but I believed them."

"Somebody has to know," I said, realizing that I'd growled out the words.

"Who? I asked over half of the gangsters in Chicago."

"You didn't ask the right one."

Christian gave me a look, and then raised his finger. "No."

"Yes. We need to ask Capone."

"Umm, no. One," he held up his finger. "We're supposed to stay away from Capone on Ness's orders. Two," he put up a second finger. "Why would Capone know? Three," a third finger joined the others. "If he did, why would he bother to tell *us*? He could just go deal with Moira on his own. He doesn't need us."

I shrugged. I had an idea why Capone would help us, but I didn't want to tell Christian just yet. I didn't want him saying no and backing out. This was about saving Sarah. "You've asked everyone else. It's only natural for us to go to the top and ask the man in charge."

Christian sighed and stood up, placing the crucifix into his pocket. "I know I'm going to regret this." He walked to his coat stand and grabbed his hat. "But let's go see Capone."

Chapter 24

We headed downstairs and got into Christian's car. As he started the motor, I noticed that the windscreen had been repaired. My anger bubbled up again, "You couldn't find my sister, but you had time to fix your damn car?"

"For your information, getting the windscreen replaced was the excuse that I needed to stay out of the office yesterday. Otherwise, I would have been under Ness's watchful eye all day and wouldn't have had anything to tell you."

"You didn't have anything to tell me," I said, my anger ebbing away, but only just a bit.

"True. But I did get my car repaired." He started the motor, which coughed to life, and we headed to the Lexington Hotel. I stayed quiet on the drive, trying to keep my thoughts on getting what I needed from Capone, and not on what Moira might be doing to Sarah.

Christian parked a block away, and we walked to the hotel. The lobby was filled with guests and several men that I knew worked for Capone. They all gave us pointed glances as we walked across the lobby to the elevators.

Two goons stood by the elevators. As soon as we approached, one put a hand into his jacket while the other stepped up.

"I think you're in the wrong place, Mac." He put his hand on my chest. *As if that could stop me.* I could smell his arrogance, and I heard his heart beating a bit faster. He was hoping that I'd try something.

I smiled, and I don't know what I did, but he pulled his hand away and took a step back. A different smell rolled off of him like cheap cigar smoke. Fear.

Huh, I need to practice that in a mirror to know what I'm doing.

"We're here to see your boss," Christian said.

The goon walked over to a telephone and picked up the receiver. His friend never took his eyes off of us, and he kept his hand inside his jacket.

"It's Johnny. I got two G-men down here wanting to see the boss."

I could make out the reply from the other end. "Keep them there. I'll be down in a minute."

The goon put down the receiver and I could see the relief in his eyes. *Man, how did I spook him so well?*

It had been less than a minute when the bell for the elevator dinged and the doors opened. Out stepped Frank Nitti.

"You're looking good after your close shave," I said.

"We'd like to see your boss," Christian said, more deferentially than I would have.

Nitti sneered at me, but looked at Christian. "Mr. Capone doesn't want to see you. You and your Kike dog can take a hike."

I shrugged, ignoring the insult. "Fine. Just tell him that we'll be happy to hold on to the property that *you* lost at the club the other night."

Nitti's face knitted itself into a scowl, and I could hear his teeth grinding. "Wait here," he said.

Nitti got into the elevator. The door closed, and the arrow showed that it was going up to the fifth floor, where Nitti would hopefully tell Capone. Christian grabbed my sleeve and jerked his head toward the lobby. "What in the name of our Blessed Father are you doing?" he hissed, keeping his voice low.

"I'm getting us in to see Capone."

"But you can't give the ledger to Capone. We don't have it, and Ness won't give it up."

"I don't care about the ledger, Ness, or Capone. I only want to save my sister. If giving Capone the damn ledger lets me do that, then so be it."

Christian shook his head, and I heard him mutter, "You are going to be the death of me."

The elevator dinged again, and I turned my head to see Nitti gesturing for us to enter. "You keep saying that," I said, quietly, to Christian. "But it hasn't happened yet."

"There's still time," he said, as we got into the elevator.

Nitti was quiet as we went up to the fifth floor. The elevator stopped, and the doors opened. Nitti led us down the hall to the office where I'd met Capone last year. We entered the outer sitting room, but we had to wait, as two thugs carried a body out of Capone's office. I recognized the bum who'd been Mr. Brown's eyes outside the speakeasy.

Nitti led us into Capone's office. Capone wore a pale green silk shirt with a dark blue tie. His face was flush, and he was taking his seat at his desk, dabbing at his lips with a monogrammed handkerchief. I could smell fresh blood, and I suddenly had a hunger that I had to fight to hold back. Nitti closed the door, but he stayed in the room.

Capone tucked the handkerchief away and leaned back in his chair, placing one hand on the desk. One of his rings flashed in the light as he tapped his fingers. "Mr. Nitti tells me that you want to make a deal. I hope you are offering more than a stupid ledger." He made a dismissive gesture with his hand. "You tricked me once before with that ruse. It will not work a second time."

As I stood there, I realized that my 'sense' of Capone was now different. The tingling sensation was less pronounced than it had been in our previous meetings. *Is this part of Joe's power? Does Capone sense anything different about me?* I studied his face, looking for any clue, but he gave nothing away.

"If that was true," I said, "you wouldn't have seen us."

"Maybe I'm just bored, Mr. Imbierowicz. It brings me pleasure to tweak your nose and watch you twist in the wind."

"Or you know that the only way to get your ledger back is through us, and you need to have your ego stroked some first," I countered.

"I do love a good ego-stroking," Capone started, and then impatiently continued. "But get to the point, Mr. Imbierowicz."

"I know who Mr. Brown's master is," I said.

"And why would I care about that?" Capone pointed a finger at me. "You took care of Mr. Brown." *Did I hear a note of appreciation in his voice?* "And Brown's so-called master is not a threat to me."

"Don't play games," Christian said. "You do care, and I think you want to know."

"Silence!" Capone snarled at Christian. "Know your place. This is a concern only for the Enlightened."

I could almost smell the smoke coming off of Christian.

"If you've come to barter with Mr. Brown's master's name," Capone said, his attention back on me, "then you will be disappointed, Mr. Imbierowicz. I already know who she is." He leaned forward in his chair and his facial scar stood out. "I've told you before that Chicago is *my* town."

He stabbed the desk with a finger. "Nothing happens here that I don't know about."

"I wasn't going to barter with Moira's name," I said coolly. "I already told you what I was offering."

"The ledger that Nitti so carelessly dropped at the speakeasy," Christian said, defying Capone's command to stay silent.

Capone shot a look to Nitti before saying, "So? I told you that the ledger means nothing to me."

I saw Christian smile out of the corner of my eye. "You keep acting like you don't care about the ledger, but you know that it will bring down you and your whole organization. And you know that we can put you away for good with what's in there, just like we did to your brother, Ralph. We've already cracked your code and, with it, we will connect you to all of the ill-gotten money you've ever earned."

I kept my face as blank as I could. *Had we broken the code?* If we hadn't, and I slipped up, Capone would know, and Christian's bluff—*was it a bluff?*—would be called.

"You think I'm afraid of the tax man?" Capone asked. "You can't collect legal taxes from illegal money." He sat back in his chair and gave a self-satisfied smile.

Christian gave a non-committal shrug. "You may not be afraid of the IRS, but I know what you *are* afraid of."

"Ha! Get a load of this mug," Capone said to Nitti. "Go ahead, whelp. Illuminate me. What am I afraid of?" Capone held out both hands wide.

"Losing power," Christian said. "Even if you win against the IRS, we'll have dragged you through so much muck that every two-bit gangster and bootlegger will know that you're vulnerable. Nobody will respect you, and you'll have to fight off every thug looking to prove themselves."

"And I'll beat all of them!" Capone snarled, his scar

turning white from his anger.

"At what cost?" I asked, picking up on Christian's thread. "You'll have already lost face, lost respect. Nobody will take Al Capone seriously ever again." I paused for a moment. "But we're offering a way for you to keep your power."

Capone leaned back, straightening his tie in an effort to compose himself. "And what do you want from me in exchange for the ledger?"

"I want to know where Moira is hiding."

"Why? I can deal with that bitch any time I want."

"She took something from me, and I want it back."

"It must be important to you, for you to come to me for help. What could possibly be so important?"

I paused for a moment, hesitant to give Capone any possible leverage.

Don't tell him, Dad said. *You can't trust what he'll do with that knowledge.*

But I've got to save Sarah, I countered. *Even if it means giving him an advantage over me.*

"Family is important," I said, using the phrase that Capone had used on me at our meeting over a year before. Capone gave the barest of nods to acknowledge the statement, but waited for me to make my point. "She took my sister, and I will make Moira pay for that."

Capone stared at me, clearly thinking. After nearly a minute, he pointed at me. "Bring me the ledger tomorrow morning, and I'll tell you where you can find Moira."

Chapter 25

"Ness is going to kill us when he finds out that the ledger is missing," Christian said, as we entered the Federal Building downtown.

"I'll worry about my job once we've saved Sarah," I said.

"No. I mean he'll actually kill us. He's been working so long to take down Capone, and now he's got the evidence that he needs in order to do it. And we're going to steal it and give it back to Capone? Ness won't bother firing us."

I shrugged. It wasn't due to the fact that I was a vampire and I knew that it would be hard for Ness to harm me. I was willing to take whatever risk, to give up my own life, if I had to, in order to save my sister's life.

We took the back stairs up to the floor where our office was located. I paused on the landing. "You don't have to do this," I told Christian. "Go home. I'll tell Ness that this was all my doing when he finds out."

Christian paused with his hand on the doorknob. I could see his grip tighten on the knob. He turned to look at me. "I'm your partner, and we're in this together. Let's get the ledger so we can save your sister."

He pulled open the door and headed down the hall. I wondered for a moment about his words, as I got the impression that there was more that he'd wanted to say, but I shrugged it off and headed after him.

The lights to our office were off, and Christian used his key to unlock the door. We made our way to Ness's office at the back of the room. The office smelled like Cloonan had spilled an entire bottle of his damn aftershave everywhere. I wrinkled my nose and blew out air to try to get rid of the smell. Then, as Christian turned the knob on Ness's door, I heard it: a faint lub-thub of a heartbeat coming from inside the office.

"Christian—" I started to say, as the door opened and the lamp on Ness's desk clicked on. The light was harsh in the dark office. Ness sat at his desk, pulling his hand back from the lamp. The expression on his face was a mixture of sadness and anger.

"Come in, gentlemen." His voice was even, conversational.

Christian and I stepped into the office. I didn't bother to close the door. Ness being here didn't change anything, but leaving the door open might give me an edge if I needed to make a quick getaway.

"You haven't been at work since the shootout at the speakeasy," Ness said to me. "Are you going to tell me where you've been?"

"I had to meet a friend," I said.

"Out of town?"

I don't know how he knew, but it didn't matter. Sarah was the only thing that mattered right now. Playing word games with Ness wouldn't help her. "Yes." I defiantly stuck my chin out a bit.

"After you went to see your parents," Ness continued. "Against *my* orders."

"I went there to *protect* my parents!" I shouted. Acid ate at my stomach and I felt a surge of adrenalin. I had to concentrate hard just to keep my fangs from extending.

"Moira attacked me at my apartment," I continued, stepping up to the desk. I was looming over Ness, my body screaming to take action. "She threatened my family and I went to protect them."

Ness just stared at me, his expression unchanged, though his eyes had widened a bit at my outburst. I felt a hand on my elbow and a gently cooling sensation flowed up my arm.

"Saul, take it easy," Christian said.

I hadn't realized that my heart had been racing and that my hands had clenched into fists. I looked down and saw blood. I opened my palms and saw the wounds that were caused by my claws—*wait, I have claws?*—healing. My nails were also returning to normal, but they'd been thick, sharp claws a moment before. The shock did more to calm me down than Christian's words had.

Ness hadn't seen my hands, or perhaps he was unfazed by the change. (I doubt it was the latter. Even I had been surprised by this new revelation.) "And what are you two doing here this late?" Ness asked.

"I came to get the ledger," I said, keeping my anger in check, but tired of dancing around the reason. "But you already knew that, since you were waiting for us."

Ness acknowledged this with a small bow of his head. "It's not yours to have, Saul. It is the property of Uncle Sam now."

My whole body tensed, and I found myself clenching my hands into fists again. "You don't understand," I said, through gritted teeth. "I need it to save Sarah."

"Sarah?"

"His sister," Christian said, placing his hand on my elbow again. The same cooling sensation flowed through me. "Moira kidnapped her," he continued. "We need the ledger to find out where Moira has taken her."

"From Capone," Ness said, with a sigh. He looked at me, and I saw the sadness in his eyes. "I'm sorry, Saul. This case is too important. Stopping Capone is more important than your sister. I won't give you the ledger."

I almost couldn't control it this time. I wanted to fling the desk aside and tear the words from Ness's throat. Not even Christian's touch had an effect on me.

Then do it for me, nudnik, Sarah said. *If I find out that you killed your boss in order to save me, then I'm gonna be really pissed.*

He's just doing his job, Saul, Dad added. *You'd hurt him—kill him—just for doing his job? Don't be a* schlemiel.

If you'd rather break your poor mother's heart, Mom piled the guilt on. *Then do this. Be a monster worse than that Mr. Capone to save your sister. I'm sure God will understand.*

My anger flowed away as quickly as it had come. "I don't want to take it by force," I said, surprising myself with how even it sounded, and how much scarier it sounded because of it. "But I will if I have to. I will get it, and I will find out where Moira is hiding. Nobody is going to stop me from saving Sarah."

Chapter 26

"I'm not nobody, you damn Kike blood-sucker."

Christian and I turned to see a man standing in the doorway. I hadn't heard him come up and, while I was surprised that I hadn't heard him, I was even more surprised by who was standing there. I recognized him from his photos in the papers.

J. Edgar Hoover.

He wore a dark suit, the corner of a handkerchief sticking up from the breast pocket. His face was long and narrow, with close-cropped black hair and the beginnings of a receding hairline.

"Mr. Hoover, sir," Christian said, the deference clear in his voice. To me he added, "Mr. Hoover is my boss. He oversees the Night Watchers."

I knew that Hoover ran the Bureau of Investigations. Every man, woman, and child in America knew that. It shouldn't have surprised me that Hoover also ran the Night Watchers.

Hoover gave a sharp nod. "The Night Watchers keep an eye on all sorts of monsters and other things, including vampires." He squinted as he said the last word, and glared at me. "Mr. Ness has been keeping an eye on *you* for me, in addition to Capone."

"Keeping an eye on *me*?" I asked, glancing back to Ness. "But I work for him. I'm one of the good guys."

Hoover gave a small chuckle, but his expression made it seem like I was the funniest thing since *Amos 'n' Andy*.

"Ness is correct," Hoover said. "The ledger belongs to us now, and nobody will get their hands on it. Monster or not, I've waited a long time to get Capone. I'm not going to let some pissant Jew vampire take it and screw up our best chance at taking down the country's most notorious gangster."

"And what about my sister?" I asked, through gritted teeth. I was doing my best to not rip the head off of American's number one law enforcement officer.

"If she's not dead already, then we'll deal with her at a later date," Hoover said.

I tried to absorb what he was saying, the implication of his words. From the moment that I'd seen Moira's note on Sarah's pillow, I had known what the possible outcomes might be, but I hadn't wanted to give them credence, as if just thinking about it would make it happen. Now, Hoover had just blurted out my deepest fears about what Moira was going to do to my sister.

But, before I could say anything, Hoover said, "I'm pulling both of you off of the Capone case immediately. You no longer work for Ness. I'm reassigning the two of you directly to the Night Watchers."

"You can't do that," I said. I was reacting more to what this meant for me to save my sister, rather than being taken off of Ness's team.

"I'm the top cop in this country," Hoover said, "And I can do anything I damn well please."

I noticed that Christian was hanging his head, apparently accepting Hoover's orders without question.

"I'll quit," I said. "I won't go work for you if it means I can't save Sarah."

Hoover pierced me with his eyes. "Fine, quit, but the only reason that I haven't had one of my men shove a stake through your heart is that you work for the government. You quit, and I'll make sure that you get what you deserve before you leave this building."

My eyes widened at the threat, and I cast a glance at Christian. He wouldn't meet my gaze. I didn't know if that meant that he'd follow Hoover's orders and kill me, or if he'd refuse because of our special bond.

"Look, son," Hoover softened his voice, trying to mollify me. "I get that you want to save your sister, but she's been with this Moira for too long already. You have to accept the reality of the situation."

I fought back the bile that was creeping up my throat and the tears filling my eyes. "You're wrong," I said, my voice hoarse. "There's still a chance to save her."

Hoover shook his head. He turned to Christian. "There's another threat in Chicago. I need you and Saul to look into it. Evaluate the danger to the city and remove the threat if you can. Ness and his team will handle Capone."

Chapter 27

Ever since Hoover had stepped into the office, my anger had been seething just under the surface. Now, it boiled over. "You don't get it!" I snarled. I felt my face changing, my fangs growing. "I'll do whatever I have to do to save Sarah, even if it means taking the ledger from your dead hands!"

All of my senses were on edge. I heard and felt the beating of three hearts. Multiple scents overwhelmed my nose: the cloying aftershave from the outer office, stale cigar smoke and cigarettes, and fear mixed with adrenaline. I heard the rustle of Christian's coat as he pulled it open to reach for something. I heard the scratch of wood from the desk and the smell of gun oil, followed by the cocking of a gun. I ignored what my senses were trying to tell me, focusing my anger and fury at Hoover. I wanted him to react. I wanted him to cower in fear at what I truly had become. I would kill him if I needed to, but I hoped to scare him enough to get what I wanted without me having to do that. But, through all of this, whatever Ness and Christian were doing, and my transformation into the monster that I was, Hoover just stood there, with a smug look on his face. He wasn't the least bit scared of me, and his reaction made me pause.

Then I felt a burning pain on my hand. I looked down to see Christian touching a crucifix to me. I pulled my hand away with a jerk, "What the hell?"

"It was either that, or let Ness put a bullet through your head," Christian said. He pointed behind me with the silver crucifix. I turned my head to see Ness standing with his service revolver pointed directly at my head. His gaze was steady, his hand was a rock. I wasn't afraid, I could survive the shot—I think—but the sudden realization that my boss was willing to shoot me made my blood run cold.

I pulled out one of the chairs that was in front of the desk and sat down. I put my head in my hands. *I've failed.*

It's okay, Saul, Sarah said. *I'd hate myself if you got killed trying to save me.*

I can't lose both of my children, Mom added. *Besides, I just got my little boy back. I can't go through that again.*

You listen to Mr. Hoover, Dad declared. *He's a very smart man.*

"What is this new threat?" I heard Christian ask. I didn't bother to look up or join the discussion. *What's the point?*

"I can't say for sure," Hoover said. I looked up at Ness and rolled my eyes. He ignored me. "And that's why I need you and Saul."

I turned in the chair to stare at Hoover. "My attention on things that go bump in the night is not solely focused on vampires masquerading as gangsters and wannabe G-men in the Windy City," he deigned to acknowledge me with a nod.

"Down in Louisiana there was a voodoo priestess we've been watching."

"Was?" I asked, unable to stay out of the conversation. Hoover turned his gaze on me.

"I've had a pair of agents—Night Watchers—watching this woman for a couple of years. She's a witch. She's known as Kalfu and, if the rumors are to be believed, she's over one hundred years old."

Kalfu? Kalfu? Why does that name sound familiar?

"My agents went missing about a year ago. They didn't check in. I sent a couple more men to check on them. Both agents were dead—their bodies had withered into dried husks—and Kalfu had disappeared. We think she came to Chicago."

"Why Chicago?" asked Ness.

Kalfu in Chicago? The name was stuck in my head like a piece of food caught in my teeth.

"We've had some sightings, some inklings that she may have come north. She might have arrived here about a year ago."

Then it clicked, like placing the final piece of a puzzle. *Moira.* She'd mentioned the name. When I'd spied on her and Mr. Brown, Moira had mentioned doing Kalfu's dirty work. *Moira knows Kalfu.*

"That's why I need Saul and Christian," Hoover said, "to find this voodoo witch and see what she's up to. What is she doing here in Chicago?"

There was a moment of silence in the office. Then I said, "I know how to find Kalfu."

Chapter 28

Hoover narrowed his eyes until they almost met in the middle. "How in the hell do you know Kalfu?"

"I don't," I said.

Hoover snorted, the sound loud in Ness's office. It was clear what he was thinking; I was trying to put one over on him. I gave him a thin smile.

"Kalfu is just a name I heard," I waited a beat, "from Moira."

That got everyone's attention. I heard a gasp from Christian and an intake of breath from Ness. Hoover did his best to keep his expression neutral, but I caught the widening of his pupils and heard an increase in his heart rate.

"Moira works with Kalfu. I know that Moira has been doing jobs for Kalfu, and I know that Brown's stunt of shooting up Capone's car was not approved by Kalfu." I spoke confidently, though I was making some educated guesses since I'd only caught part of Moira and Brown's conversation. It sounded good, and I had gotten Hoover's attention.

"Moira knows Kalfu, and she knows how to find her," I said.

"And why in the hell is a vampire working with a voodoo priestess?" Hoover asked.

I shrugged, "Sorry, that didn't come up when I was spying on them, and I couldn't just ask them, but does it matter why? If you need to find Kalfu, then we just need to find Moira."

"And to find Moira," Christian said, taking up my point, "we need to give Capone back his ledger."

I nodded, and I could hear Hoover grinding his teeth. "Capone is the only one in Chicago who knows where Moira is hiding."

"How in the hell does Capone know?" spat Hoover. "Did he give you any proof that he knows, or that he'd tell you the truth? He's a goddamn gangster. How can you trust anything that he says?"

"If we had proof," Christian said, ignoring Hoover's blasphemy, "then we wouldn't be here."

"Capone's got an ego the size of Lake Michigan," Ness said. I was surprised that he was taking our side. "He's always boasted that nothing happens in Chicago that he doesn't know about."

"Capone has his ways," I said. I remembered the bum that had been carried out of Capone's office: the same bum that had been a procurator for Mr. Brown. What information had Capone taken from that man before he had killed him? How many anonymous eyes and ears of his own does Capone have throughout the city? How many procurators could a vampire have at any one time? As usual, I didn't know the answers, but I didn't need to know, exactly. Mr. Brown and Moira had both used them, so Capone probably did, too. "He knows. And his price to give us that information is his ledger."

Hoover's mouth was a thin line. He stuck his hand up to his chin and stared at the floor. I looked over at Christian, who gave a subtle shrug. Finally, he looked up to Ness, and gave the barest of nods.

Ness put his gun down, and walked over to a safe that

was sitting in the corner. The clicking of the wheel as Ness spun the combination sounded like the patter of rain, but I was disappointed that I couldn't hear the tumblers click into place. Ness opened the safe, pulled something out, and then closed the door and spun the dial.

He stood up and set the ledger down on his desk. "We've already broken Capone's code. There's enough information in here," he tapped the cover, "to tie Capone to a lot of illegal money."

"Money he's never paid a dime in taxes on," Hoover said. He gave another small nod, and Ness picked up the ledger and handed it to Christian. Christian took it without a word.

"Wait," I said. "A minute ago, you were willing to let my sister die so you could keep the ledger. Now you're just going to give it to us? You know we're going to give it to Capone."

Ness nodded. "We've already had the entire ledger photographed and had the process witnessed by two lawyers."

"A judge will accept that we won't want to produce the real ledger out of an abundance of caution," Hoover added. "We wouldn't want Capone to steal his evidence back." He gave a sardonic grin.

"Then why in the hell didn't you give it to us right away?" I asked, the frustration starting to transform into anger. I'd been willing to kill them to get the ledger, and now they were just handing the damn thing over.

"Because Mr. Hoover needed us to commit to finding Kalfu for him," Christian said.

What? That made no sense to me. "You could have just asked!" I said.

"When you earn something, you are more committed to the task than when you are just given it," Hoover said with a smug smile. I couldn't believe it, and shook my head. Platitudes and fake wisdom to make a damn point. This was crazy. This entire event wasn't about keeping the ledger from us, it was about letting Hoover show us that he was the one in charge.

Fuck it, let them play their stupid game. I still have time to save Sarah. I stood up and took the ledger from Christian, and then headed to the door.

Hoover stepped aside. I was halfway across the main office when Hoover said, "I don't give a rat's ass what happens to Moira or your sister. Just find out where Kalfu is hiding. That's the only reason I'm letting you do this."

Chapter 29

It was after midnight when we left the Federal Building. We got into Christian's car, and it started with a reluctant cough. He pulled out and took the first right.

"Uh, the Lexington is that way," I said, pointing out the back.

"We're not going there," he said.

"We're not? Then why'd we just go through all of that back there with Ness and Hoover to get this?" I lifted the ledger off my lap.

"We need a plan," Christian said. "For once."

"I've always had plans," I said, a bit testily.

"Okay, then we need a *good* plan," Christian countered. "For once."

I wanted to say something, but he was right. "So, where are we going?"

"Your place," Christian said, turning onto State Street. "I don't want to go to Capone's unprepared. I don't trust him, and even if he gives us what we want, do you think for one moment that you won't go running off after your sister right then?"

I acknowledged his point with a sigh. Christian was absolutely right. The car slowed, and he pulled into a parking space in front of the Chicago Theater.

"You need to feed," he said, getting out of the car. "You need to be at full strength when we go after Moira.

"I feel fine," I said, as I climbed out of the car. "I fed earlier today."

Christian shook his head, rolled his eyes, and then tapped his wrist. He crossed the street.

Oh, he meant feed on him. After feeding on Joe, I hadn't thought about feeding on Christian again, but it made sense. I'd get some needed strength, and our bond was always strongest after I fed on Christian's blood.

I crossed the street after him, and we went up to my apartment. The place was still a mess from my fight with Moira, and Christian just shook his head.

"Sorry, I had to let the maid go," I said.

I heard a sniff from Christian that I took as a laugh. He went into the kitchen and pulled out a glass, and then he sat down at the table and rolled up his sleeve. I tossed the ledger onto my armchair.

"This would be faster if you'd just let me feed on you directly," I said.

Christian ignored me and continued to prepare his kit. From the many pockets of his coat, he pulled out a short rubber tube and a metal box that I knew contained a glass syringe and needle. "Why do you always bring this up?" he asked. "Once was enough."

"What if our bond is from me *actually* feeding, and not just drinking your blood?"

"I doubt that, otherwise our bond would have stopped working last year."

"It might," I said.

"I'm willing to take that risk," Christian said. He proceeded to draw out a full syringe of his blood. It wasn't a lot—it never was—and I think that was also part of Christian's plan: only giving me the bare minimum, and maybe a bit of payback for my almost draining him in Atlantic City.

But it always seemed to do the trick, even though it was just barely a swallow. As he finished up, I idly wondered how other vampires did this. I was sure that Capone didn't let Nitti draw out a syringe of his blood for Capone to feed on. But at the same time, there was that "special vintage" that Capone had shared at his dinner party last year. How did he get it? Did they drain the procurator after his death to keep it on hand? How long did the blood last? *Even more questions I will never know the answers to.*

Christian finished up, squirting the blood into a glass. The smell hit me instantly, and I found my mouth watering. Christian handed me the glass. "Bottoms up," I said, draining the blood like it was a highball. It tasted sweet on my tongue, and I noted a distinct flavor that differed from the other people I had recently fed upon. *Was that just a part of our bond, or do people have flavors?*

As I set the glass down, I felt a sudden tingling at the nape of my neck. "Someone is here," I said, as there came a knock on the door. Christian gave an involuntary shudder as he also felt the vampire.

I hesitated a moment, and Christian said, "Whoever it is knows that you're here."

I felt a little sheepish as I went to the door. I opened it up, and my head swam for a moment from déjà vu. Al Capone stood in the hallway wearing a starched white shirt, black dinner jacket, and a glossy black bow tie. He smiled, the movement causing his scar to stand out. His face was flush, and I smelled cigarettes, whiskey, and blood.

"Good evening, Mr. Imbierowicz," Capone greeted me. "I was enjoying a night at the opera when a little rat informed me that you'd gotten my ledger." He tapped the side of his temple. "May I come in so that we can transact our business?"

I hesitated, my mind going back to that night nearly a year ago when Capone had forced me into my neighbor's apartment, right across the hall from me. I'd had a new neighbor, a banker or stockbroker or something—I'd never gotten to know the man—who'd moved out sometime after the Crash in October. The place was empty now. My landlord had been unable to find a tenant as people continued to lose their jobs.

"I'm perfectly happy to discuss things here in the hallway," Capone held his hands wide, "where your neighbors can hear everything." It was well after midnight, but I still heard an intake of breath from one of my other neighbors—a middle-aged woman and her husband lived there—and I saw a shadow move under the door.

I didn't want to give Capone access to my apartment, and I was a bit disgusted with myself that Capone was using the same tactic on me that I had used on my father, but I wanted to find Moira and Sarah even more. I'd have to deal with letting Capone have his access later.

"Please come in, Mr. Capone," I swung my arm to usher him inside, and another titter of déjà vu tickled my memory.

Capone stepped into my apartment, and I closed the door. "Is there any way to take back an invitation after it's given?" I asked.

Capone turned and gave me a smile. "If there was, why would I tell you that, now that I have access to your humble abode?" He again held out his hands, turning in a small circle. A smirk jerked at his lips as he took in the apartment. I could see his eyes flicker to the bloodstain on the floor, and to a couple of pearls from Moira's broken strand.

"It looks like you've been entertaining," Capone said. "Moira, I assume." His toe kicked a single pearl, which rolled under the armchair in the living room. He turned his gaze on me, his voice hard. "Our deal still stands, even if you've found out where Moira is hiding on your own."

"I entertained Moira the other night," I said, my words causing a smile to flicker on Capone's lips. "We still don't know where Moira has taken my sister."

Christian stood in the kitchen, leaning against the sink, as Capone and I bantered. His arms were crossed, and he glared at Capone.

"Then it's good for both of us that I have the information that you want." Capone turned to me. "Now, I believe that you have *my* property. I'd like it back. *Now*." The last word was spoken in the same tone that I used in order to get others to do my bidding. I didn't feel any compulsion to get the ledger; I didn't even need to resist his command. I wasn't sure if that was because I'd fed from Joe, gaining his powers, or if Capone had just meant to be menacing.

"Not until you tell me where Moira is hiding," I said. I found myself standing up a bit. "I won't give you the ledger until you tell me."

"*Che palle*! Have you got a pair? Such bravado." Capone was laughing, but his tone was mocking. Then Capone moved. To me, it looked like he had just trotted into the kitchen, grabbed Christian's hair and pulled his head back to expose his neck, but Christian's suddenly wide eyes and raised eyebrows told me that, to him, Capone had just appeared next to him.

Damnit! I'd let Capone catch me flat-footed.

Capone's fangs grew, and his brow furrowed into his vampire mask. "Get me my fucking ledger, you Kike shit, and maybe I'll let your pet live."

It was like a fist had grabbed my heart and gave it a squeeze. Anger flowed like a river through my veins. In less than the blink of a vampire's eye, I was on Capone, my left hand tight around his neck. I then lifted him off his feet, as if he weighed nothing more than a sack of flour. Christian's expression from Capone's actions a moment ago was now reflected on Capone's face.

"You don't order me around in *my* home," I hissed. My own fangs had extended, and my brow furrowed. "You don't threaten *my* friends." I spat the words at Capone. "And you don't call me a Kike, you fucking Wop *kucker.*"

Christian pulled himself out of Capone's grasp and left the kitchen. I felt my claws digging into Capone's neck, trickles of blood flowing down toward the pure white collar. "Tell me where Moira is hiding, or I'll tear your fucking head off."

Capone had been struggling, but then I saw something change in his eyes. He tried to speak, moving his lips, trying to suck in a breath. I released my grip just a bit and lowered him until his feet touched the floor.

"Do that, Mr. Imbierowicz, and you won't find out where Moira has squirreled away your sister. Your threats are meaningless. I'm holding all the cards."

Geez, you really suck at being menacing, Sarah said.

She was right, as was Capone. I couldn't kill him if I wanted the information. I kept one hand on Capone's neck, my claws still embedded into his skin. I held out my other hand to Christian. It took a moment, but then he placed the ledger in my hand. I held the ledger up for Capone, who plucked it almost reverently from me. I applied a bit of pressure on my hand around Capone's neck.

"The Shedd," he said. "The new aquarium being built down by Soldier Field. It's supposed to open in a couple of months. Moira has been hiding there since you and your pet took care of Mr. Brown."

That gives new meaning to sleeping with the fishes, Sarah said with a laugh.

I released Capone and took a step back. Capone made a show of straightening his tie, and then touched his neck. The wounds had already healed, but his finger came away stained red. He looked at the blood there, and then his eyes met mine. He lifted the finger and sucked the blood off. His eyes never left mine and, even though I'd just held his life in my hands, I felt a shiver race up my spine. His grey eyes were cold, dead, and said that I'd just thrown away my one chance to kill him.

Capone then tucked the ledger under his arm and walked out of my apartment without another word.

Chapter 30

Christian had been right. As soon as Capone left, I insisted that we leave immediately. Christian had taken pleasure in being slow and deliberate, and the only reason that I hadn't left without him was that I needed his help. Even with Joe's blood, I knew that it would take both of us to save Sarah.

Finally, Christian was ready, and we got into his car. He backed out of his parking space, made a U-turn, and headed south toward Soldier Field and the new aquarium. It had been nearly three years since they'd broken ground for the aquarium. Most of the city had been following the progress ever since John Shedd had first decided to build the biggest and best aquarium in the world, right here in Chicago. The papers had been hyping up the grand opening, which was scheduled for the end of May. Earlier in the year, they'd brought in train cars full of salt water to fill the aquarium's many exhibits.

"I wonder if they'll have sharks," Christian ruminated, as we drove.

"What?"

"At the aquarium. I hope they have an exhibit with sharks."

"We aren't there to sightsee," I said, trying to keep my anger in check. *Since when am I the responsible one?*

"I know that. But, you know, when it opens up, it would

be interesting to go. Especially if they have sharks."

I looked at Christian, my eyes narrowed in concern. "We're going there to save Sarah," I reminded him.

"No, we're going there to learn about this voodoo priestess, where she is, what she's doing in the city, and how Moira is connected to her." Christian's voice had turned cold. He turned the car and we headed south, with Grant Park on our right, and Lake Michigan a black abyss to our left.

"*I'm* going there to save my sister," I said, and I was surprised when it came out as a growl.

"*We* have a job to do," Christian growled back.

"My family comes first."

Christian slowed and turned left, heading toward the lake. The Field Museum loomed on our right and, ahead, the new aquarium gleamed in the moonlight. The building looked like a large mausoleum.

"Your sister may already be dead, or worse," Christian said.

"No, you're wrong," I said, shaking my head. I didn't want to think about what Moira may have done. She'd only had Sarah for forty-eight hours. That wasn't enough time for Moira to do anything, was it?

It's plenty of time to kill me, Sarah reminded me.

You're not helping, I told her. *But Moira doesn't want you dead. If she did, she could have just left you laying in a bloody mess in your room. But two days isn't enough time for her to do anything else, is it? To make you into…*

A monster like you?

Yes.

How should I know? she asked. *You're the monster. How many vampires have you made so far?*

None. I was very thankful for that.

So, you have no idea how long it takes to make one. Do you even know how *to make one?*

No, I admitted to myself. Another bit of information that I was in the dark about. This time, it might have serious consequences.

Christian stopped outside the front entrance and turned off the engine. We got out, and I could see the horizon getting lighter with each minute. A breeze was blowing in off the lake, the smell of lake water wafting in with it. I could hear the waves lapping against the shore.

Christian opened the back door. I watched him, wondering what he was doing, and saw him pull on a hidden latch. He pulled down part of the back seat, revealing a hidden compartment. "Has that always been there?"

"Truesdale had it put in," he said, as he leaned into the hidden space. He emerged with a shotgun in his hands. "It allowed us to carry more firepower if we needed it, without scaring local citizens or alerting our quarry."

I gave a low whistle as I pulled out my own weapon. Christian racked a round on the shotgun, and then made the sign of the cross. "Let's go," he said.

We headed up the steps to the large entrance doors. I gave a tug; it was locked, of course.

"There might be a service—" Christian started to say.

I pulled on the door, hard. I felt the lock break with a loud CRACK.

"Lord in Heaven. Well, now they know that we're here."

"Good." I pulled open the door and went inside.

The entrance space was a wide room with stone floors and walls. A booth stood just inside where visitors would be able to buy their tickets. Massive pillars flanked an opening that led to the center of the building. Hanging from the opening was a clock with silhouettes of creatures in place of the numbers on a white clock face. To the right and left were openings to other spaces. A sign hung from each opening that said, "Gallery".

The air was humid, and I smelled salt water and fish. A lot of fish. I walked toward the center of the building, passing between the pillars and under the clock. The hands on the clock showed it was almost lobster past a frog, so just after four a.m. In the middle of the central room, plants and a small pool were surrounded by a brass rail. Additional openings led off of this central atrium, presumably to other galleries.

"Where would Moira be hiding?" Christian asked, as he stepped into the atrium.

I looked around and spotted one gallery whose entrance was blocked. A couple of sawhorses had been set up, and a paint-splattered tarpaulin had been hung in order to block any view into the gallery. A sign had been tacked to one of the sawhorses that read, "Keep Out".

"That must be it," I said, walking around the room.

"She's not very subtle, is she?"

I shrugged. My only experience with dames had been with Moira and, clearly, I had never understood her.

And you never will, love, Moira beamed.

You got that right, Sarah teased.

I ignored them both and walked around the room to reach the gallery entrance. I found the edge of the tarpaulin, pulling it aside with the barrel of my pistol.

"Huh," Christian said. I turned, and he pointed to a plaque on the wall. It read, "Shark Gallery".

"No, definitely not subtle," I said.

The gallery was dark, although I could make out large glass windows that were spaced along the walls. A brass railing ran along the perimeter of the gallery, separating visitors from the tanks. I could see light coming from the far end of the room. My sense of smell was overwhelmed by the smell of fish and saltwater, and the hum of water pumps and other mechanical noises behind the tanks seemed to be an effective mask for noise, as I could only make out indistinct voices coming from the room where the light was.

We headed toward the far end of the gallery, careful to make as little noise as possible. After a few steps, the voices started to become clearer. The gallery itself curved, creating a space that would allow us to approach without being seen. We crept forward, and I could see eyes and fins swimming behind the glass of the aquarium tanks that we passed.

"We need to go," said a gruff, male voice. Christian and I stopped, and I wondered if we'd been spotted. I felt no tingling sensation, but then again, I hadn't felt anything from Moira since I'd found out that she wasn't dead.

"We've been here too long already," the gruff voice continued. "I'm sure he knows that we're here. We can't risk getting caught."

There was no answer, and Christian and I continued forward.

"The new safe house is ready for us," said the gruff voice. Christian and I stopped again. "The surviving men from Pandora's Legacy are keeping an eye on things. Nobody will know where we've gone."

I started to move forward again, but Christian held up a hand for me to stop. He continued forward, sticking close to the inside wall to stay out of view.

"Da Queen returns tonight," said another voice. He had an accent that I couldn't place, but it was definitely not that of a native Chicagoan. "Your debt to da Queen is unpaid."

I watched Christian slip forward. He stopped, as he was within ten feet of the end of the gallery. If he came any closer, he'd be spotted.

"I know my place." It was Moira. "I have not forgotten my debt to Kalfu." She sounded both defiant and resigned.

"Tha Queen is anxious to complete her plan," a third voice said. Another one not from Chicago, but it sounded older than the first outsider. "She wants you ta be a part of it. She was promised her kingdom, and she will collect on what is owed ta her. And you will be at her side."

"Only because she's afraid of this other vampire," Moira said.

Other vampire? Kingdom? What in the hell is going on?

"Dat otha vamp is gone," said the second voice. "He might even be dead."

"Then why does Kalfu need me?" There was resignation in Moira's voice.

"Because your kind has a habit of not staying dead," said the older voice. "You are da insurance, in case he's not dead. If he's not, Kalfu needs you ta stop him."

"Fine," Moira said, still sounding resigned. "Get our guest, and let's get to the safe house." I heard footsteps and the rustling of clothes.

"You will need ta explain da girl ta da Queen," said the second voice. "She is not part of da plan. Da Queen is not happy that she is with you."

Girl? Sarah! I moved forward.

"And how does Kalfu know about her?" Moira asked, with anger in her voice. "I know you haven't been in contact with her. Not in the past two days."

"Tha Queen will not be happy about tha girl," said the older voice. "You work for tha Queen. You take orders from her. You do not get ta decide things for yourself."

"Yes, I may work for Kalfu," Moira said, acid on her tongue. "But she doesn't dictate orders to me. Not in this regard." That sounded like the old Moira I had known, full of *chutzpah*.

I stood next to Christian, who glared at me. I should have stayed back, because if there were any vampires, we were close enough that they could feel me, and vice versa. That's why Christian had gone ahead of me, as he could feel the vampires, but he was invisible to them. But I knew that Moira was different. Her presence did something to mask the presence of other vampires. It had happened with Mr. Brown, as we'd not been able to feel each other under Pandora's Legacy.

I heard a sigh from around the bend, and I assumed that it was coming from Moira. "Let's go," she said.

I panicked. Could there be a door at the end of the hall that they could slip out of? We might not have a chance to confront Moira, to find out where Sarah is, to get her back. I caught Christian turning to gape at me out of the corner of my eye, but I didn't care. I wouldn't let Moira slip away. I ran around the corner and into the wide alcove that made up the end of the gallery. Lights in the ceiling and along the walls lit the area in a bright, white light. I saw six people plus Moira. Two were now clearly vampires—they were the closest to me and were turning toward me, their fangs already extended. Two stood along the back wall and wore brown overcoats over brown suits and brown shoes. *Mr. Brown wannabes.* I bet their socks and undergarments were also brown. They were slower than the vampires, but they were reaching inside their coats, most likely for their guns. The last two people were tall black men. They seemed ordinary enough—I was sure that they were not vampires—but I was also sure that they were dangerous in their own right. One of the men stood closest to Moira. He was broad-shouldered, with powerful arms and a shaved head. He looked like he could have outhit Josh Gibson and outfought Jack Dempsey. The other man wore glasses and had an aged top hat perched on the top of his head. He carried an ebony cane that was topped with a silver top piece. The man himself was as aged as the top hat that he wore, with deep wrinkles and age spots giving character to his face.

I noticed all of this out of the corners of my eyes as I looked directly at Moira. She stood with her back to me, looking at my reflection in the large windows in the wall. She wore a long, red leather coat, her pale red hair flowing over a turned-up collar.

Something moved in the windows, and I realized that it was the glass front to a large aquarium. The two windows took up nearly the entire back wall, and there was no exit door that would have allowed Moira and her party to make an escape. I also didn't see Sarah, and my stomach clenched as I wondered where Moira was keeping my sister.

A shape floated by one of the windows, and then passed in front of Moira. It was a long, sleek shape with jagged fins jutting from its sides, back, and tail. It was a dull grey color, though I could make out stripes of a darker grey along its flanks. The shark jerked away from Moira, and then circled to the back of the tank.

Moira slowly turned around, her bright green eyes looking at me through strands of her hair. Her pale skin was offset by the bright red lipstick that she wore. The coat was open, and she had on a black skirt that fell just past her knees, and a white blouse. A red scarf was wrapped around her neck. A coquettish smile played across her lips.

"Hello, Saul," she said. "It's about time you arrived." Her voice was full of confidence, and something else... Pleasure? The resignation I heard in her voice just a couple of minutes ago had completely vanished.

Chapter 31

I was aware of many things at once. The two vampires were standing on the balls of their feet, their knees bent slightly, as though they were getting ready to pounce, like lions on a gazelle. Christian stepped into view, his shotgun leveled. The Mr. Brown twins pulled Tommy Guns from under their overcoats. The man in the top hat placed his cane in front of him, both hands casually resting on the silver top. His companion gave a broad smile, and cracked his knuckles. In the center, as if she was a spider sitting within her web, was Moira.

I couldn't sense her; she was a blank spot in the room, but she had grabbed all of my attention. She stood with her hands on her hips, and a slight smile on her lips. Her green eyes sparkled, as if she'd been waiting for this moment.

Despite our last encounter, I was enthralled with her. I don't know why she had this power over me, but my gun remained pointed at the floor, and my fangs stayed tucked away.

Why does she have this power over me?

Duh, Sarah's voice taunted me. *Because guys only think with their putz.*

Sarah!

I forced myself to stop looking longingly at Moira like I was on my first date with her, and actually looked at her. The white blouse she wore made her skin look ashen. Her cheeks were hollow, and her eyes were sunken, creating deep shadows that she tried to hide with makeup, but it only made the changes stand out more. I realized that Moira looked like a walking corpse. I mean, even more like a corpse than normal.

"Where's my sister?" I growled, finally releasing my fangs. "Where's Sarah?"

Moira laughed, a sound that I remembered well, and it seemed to cut some of the tension in the room. "Oh, Saul, I love it when you get all *manly*." She mimicked the growl with one of her own, and stepped forward. "Your dear, sweet sister belongs to me now."

"No! What have you done to her? If you've hurt her, in any way, I will kill you."

"Ooh... so violent," she crooned, smirking. She lifted a red-painted nail to her mouth and tapped her lips. The leather bracelet was too big for her wrist, and it slid down onto her forearm, the white stones standing out sharply against her skin. "There's something different about you, Saul. I kinda like it."

"Show me Sarah or I'll show you just how different I've become." I felt my forehead change, and claws extended from my fingers.

"Perfect," Moira said. "There's one chance for you to save your sister, and your parents."

Some of my anger ebbed as I grasped at the life preserver of hope that she'd just tossed me. "What?"

"I said that you can save your sister."

"But... you just said..."

"I needed to see what sort of a reaction I'd get. I needed to see just how committed you really are."

"Saul, she's playing you," Christian said, from behind me. This drew the attention of Moira's two vampires.

I ignored Christian. "Committed?"

"How committed you'd be to saving your sister. Because I knew that, if you were truly committed, you'd do anything to save her."

"I am," I said, without hesitation. I heard Christian actually swear, under his breath.

"Good." Moira gave me a smile. "It's very simple, Saul. To save your sister, I need you to join me."

"What?"

"Oh, Saul," Moira giggled. "You were always a bit slow on the uptake. I need a partner, a right-hand man, so to speak. After you took my Brian away from me, I need someone to help me."

"I won't—" I started to say, but Moira cut me off.

"Won't? You said you'd do anything, *anything*, to save your sister. I need you to fill the role that I created for you in the first place."

"I…" My mind was floundering, as if I was one of these fish that was swimming around me, and I had just been pulled from the tank and tossed onto the floor. I had a chance to save Sarah and my parents from any harm (from Moira, at least). But to do it, I'd have to cross the final step on my journey, and become the monster that I had been trying to avoid becoming since I woke up in my apartment last year, after Capone had killed me. I had no illusions that that's what I'd be if I joined with Moira. I knew that I'd have to lose any shred of my humanity that was left.

"It's a simple decision," said Moira.

"Saul, don't do it," hissed Christian. "She's baiting you. She's just using you."

"Join me, Saul. I'll let your sister go, and then we can take down Capone, together. That's all you've ever really wanted, isn't it?"

I'd made up my mind, and I was about to tell Moira 'yes' when I felt it: the tingling that indicated that other vampires were nearby. I saw Moira's eyes widen, a sneer curling her lips.

A man's voice said, "Here we are, all together. Just like old times."

Chapter 32

I turned around to see Al Capone. He was striding purposefully down the gallery, like he owned the place. He'd changed out of his tuxedo, and instead wore a silver-grey suit with a powder blue shirt and a dark red tie. A snap-brimmed fedora sat on his head.

I saw movement behind him, but I couldn't make out who was there. Capone was momentarily distracted by one of the fish tanks, and he leaned across the rail and tapped the glass with a knuckle. He turned back, and continued down the gallery toward us. Christian had initially aimed his shotgun at Capone, but then wavered and pointed it back toward Moira. I sensed Moira's two vampires moving into a better position so that they could attack Capone. The twins also shifted their guns to point them at Capone.

"You shouldn't be surprised. I've always told you," Capone said, "that nothing happens in my town that I don't know about."

He looked to Moira, and there was the slightest shake of his head. "I don't make many mistakes, and I am not a perfect man. I have my flaws. One of them is that I am too compassionate. My heart is just too big for my own good."

I snorted in derision, and I heard another snort from behind me that matched my own. Christian actually gave a sharp, short bark of a laugh. Capone ignored us all.

"You were such a sorry creature when I found you in

that brothel. Such a pretty little thing, having to submit yourself to the scum of mankind for two minutes of humiliation."

Capone strolled closer, and read a plaque describing whatever animal lived in that particular tank. He gave a smile like he'd just learned some tidbit that he hadn't known before. He then turned his gaze back to Moira. "But I saw the ambition in your eyes when we fucked. You wanted a better life. You wanted more, like we all do. And so, in my weakness, I offered you power, wealth, and immortality."

Capone turned back from the tank. "And what did you give me in return? Did I get respect? Did I get gratitude? Did I get admiration?" He made a cutting gesture with one hand.

"No! You stabbed me in the back. I should have realized that you were too ambitious. Once you had a taste, you wanted more. You wanted it all. You weren't satisfied with everything that I gave you. What I did for you."

"What you did? For me?" Moira gave a bitter laugh. "You didn't give me anything. You made me one of your vampires, but I was still your whore. You never were going to share anything with me. So, I had to take it for myself." Moira stepped up to stand beside me, on my left.

"And now my plans are complete," she said. "I will take you down."

Capone gave a chuckle and turned to me. "I'm surprised you're going along with this, Mr. Imbierowicz. All of the trouble, all of the pain that Moira has given to you. I thought you were smarter than that."

"Moira doesn't control me," I said. "I'm only helping her to save my sister. If I can take you out of the picture, too? Well, then, that's icing on the cake in my book."

"I never understood why Moira wanted to make you

one of us," Capone spread his arms. "But now I get it." He gave a mock bow. "I applaud you dear, but I think you've bitten off more than you can chew."

"Oh, he's exactly what I need," Moira said. "And I am more than what you made me."

"What's going on?" I blurted. "I'm not anyone's servant. I'm saving Sarah."

Capone crooked his finger to one of his flunkies that was further back in the gallery, but he continued to look at me. "Nothing in Chicago escapes my notice, Mr. Imbierowicz. Nothing."

I heard footsteps and a gasp from Christian, who had a better view. Then Frank Nitti stepped up to Capone. He was leading someone else.

"Sarah!"

She was still wearing her pajamas, and had a distant, vacant expression. She was pale, and I first thought that it was a trick of the lighting, but then I saw the bite mark on her neck.

I rounded on Moira. "You said that she was safe. You said that if I joined you, she wouldn't be harmed."

Moira gave a laugh; this one was bitter and mocking. "No, Saul. I said I'd let her go. She was mine from the beginning."

"You bitch!"

I was about to slash at Moira when Capone clapped. It was a slow, mocking sound, made worse by him saying, "Bravo. Bravo. This is almost better than watching the opera."

He stepped up to Sarah and inspected her, putting a finger under her chin and lifting her face. He looked into her eyes, which were unblinking. Sarah just stood there, not moving. Behind her, Nitti had hold of Sarah by the shoulders, but not to keep her from running. I think he was keeping her on her feet. Capone nodded his head, as if he'd just confirmed something.

Capone turned back to us. "You thought you were in control. You thought you could come after me." I wasn't sure if Capone was talking to me, or if he was talking to Moira. Maybe both of us.

"You were never in control of anything, and you are not in control now. As I said, I am not a perfect man. I have my flaws. I make my mistakes. But do you know what is different about me from every other Joe on the street? I'm man enough to admit when I've made a mistake. And then, I correct that mistake."

Chapter 33

Capone snapped his fingers, and all hell broke loose. The first thing I saw was several people leaping out of the dark from behind Capone: his vampire goons. They moved fast, and they were headed for me, Moira, Moira's own goons, and Christian.

The vampires could handle themselves, as could Moira, so I jumped toward the vampire that was about to make mincemeat out of Christian. He'd yet to turn his shotgun to face the threat.

My shoulder hit the vampire, and he ricocheted away from me like a billiard ball, crashing against the wall, and busting the brass railing. He looked like he'd just been hit by a bus, and was shaking his head. My blood was up, and my claws were out. I didn't have time for this. I tore off the damaged brass rail and shoved it through the vampire's heart. Blood flowed from the wound, and then there was an explosion, as his head disappeared in a red mist.

I turned to Christian as he racked another round into the chamber, the spent shell casing clattering to the floor. He gave me a curt nod, and I took in the room.

At the back of the hall, the two black men stood close together. The older one with the top hat threw something to the ground, and a cloud of smoke erupted at their feet. Then they were gone, disappeared like Harry Houdini.

Moira's vampires were tangling with Capone's, and

Moira was busy fighting two other vampires. Her Tommy Gun-toting goons were waiving their guns back and forth, unable to shoot without hitting their friends. Up the hall, I saw Capone casually walking away, along with Nitti. But where was—

I saw Sarah on the floor along one of the walls. I pointed to her. "Go protect Sarah," I told Christian. "I'm going after Capone."

Christian ran across the hall as I took off. Capone was slipping under the tarpaulin at the entrance, followed by Nitti. I reached it in just a second and didn't hesitate, tearing the tarpaulin down. I saw Capone walking away, but Nitti had stopped next to another goon. Both had Tommy Guns in their hands, and gouts of flame were already erupting from their barrels.

I leaped back into the gallery as bullets tore past me. I heard glass shatter, as aquarium tanks spilled their watery inhabitants onto the floor. I headed back down the hall as the gunfire continued. Nitti and the other goon were walking back my way, firing as they came. The bullets continued to impact stone and glass; more tanks shattered.

Then there was a pause, as both men had to change out their drums. Their barrels smoked. I took the opportunity to slide across the floor and grabbed the first thing that I could find—a shark about two feet long—and threw it as hard as I could. At the same time, there was a shotgun blast from Christian.

Christian's shot hit the goon in the chest, and he fell to the floor. My shark missile flew toward Nitti, who panicked and fumbled his drum. It clattered to the floor as he knocked the shark aside with the barrel of his gun. The shark landed with a wet splat, and Nitti gave me a brief salute, accompanied with a sneer, as he took off.

I wanted to give chase, but Christian called to me. "You threw a shark? Why didn't you use your gun?" I looked down at the gun in my hand. I'd forgotten that I had it. I shrugged, and he jerked his gun toward the back of the gallery where fighting was still going on. Sarah's body was limp at Christian's feet.

Moira. She did that to Sarah. I wanted to get Capone, but Moira needed to pay. I ran back to the end of the gallery, just as there was a burst of gunfire from that direction. I arrived in time to see one of Capone's vampires go down in a hail of bullets as the tank behind him exploded. Water rushed out and swamped the two dead vampires—one of Moira's, and one of Capone's.

Moira had already killed one of the vampires, but she was still fighting the other one. Behind her, one of the gunmen went down as a vampire tore his throat out. The other gunman turned and fired. The bullets flew wildly, missing the vampire and glancing off the windows of the large tank with the big shark. The gun fell silent as the vampire tore out the second gunman's throat.

Now it was just Moira against the last two vampires. I wasn't going to let them kill Moira. She was for me.

I leaped into the fray, landing right next to Moira. She gave me a quick smile. "About time you joined the party."

"Where did your voodoo friends go? Don't they like to get their hands dirty?"

"They knew that I could handle this."

"That's what you call all this? Handling it?"

She gave a snort. "What about you? You just left me all alone to fend for myself."

"I was trying to stop Capone."

"And did you?" She blocked an attack from the vampire in front of her.

"No. He got away," I growled. I raised the gun and fired off several shots. The vampire in front of me jumped and weaved, and only one of my bullets hit him. The others all smacked into the glass of the large tank. The glass cracked, with long, finger-like cracks shooting away like lightning from the points of impact. A small amount of water began to trickle out.

The vampire paused, and glanced over his shoulder, then back to me. He smiled, showing long fangs. I threw the empty gun at him, but he ducked, smiling at my futile effort.

As he prepared to leap at me, there was a loud noise that came from the tank as another crack zigzagged across the surface. It was loud enough that we all stopped. Moira and the vampire facing me both turned to stare at the tank as the glass fractured, and then the tank exploded. Water gushed out in a torrent like Niagara Falls. It poured over us, knocking all of us off of our feet.

I struggled against the flow, and I stood up just in time to see the huge shark shoot out of the hole in the tank. It landed with an impact that shook the floor, and it started to flail and gnash its teeth. At that moment, the vampire in front of me started to rise, and turned in a panic to see the shark merely inches away. The vampire tried to scurry away, but couldn't get his footing. The shark's jaws snapped down on his head, tearing off half his face and all of his neck. Blood rushed from the wound, turning the water crimson.

I hustled away from the creature, turning to see Moira twist the head off of the other vampire and toss it aside. It splashed on the floor and rolled to rest against the wall.

She turned to face me, her expression unchanged as she took in the shark that was trying to eat the vampire while it also gasped for breath in the air.

"We've made a bit of a mess," I said.

Moira ran her hands through her hair, slicking off the water, and then smiled. "It's just like old times." She took a step toward me.

I shook my head and laughed, some of the stress draining away. "We never fought like this, except against each other."

"Exactly."

Chapter 34

Moira's arm moved in a flash, and I barely backed away from the attack. The white stones of the leather bracelet zipped through my vision as her hand passed less than an inch away from my throat. The tips of her fingers were jagged claws that were coated in the blood of the vampires that she'd just killed.

I counter-attacked, throwing a punch and raking my own claws across the leather of her coat, which developed a long gash as she nimbly avoided my slash. She glanced at the damage, and gave me a wicked grin. "That coat cost two hundred bucks."

"I'm surprised you paid for it."

"Oh, I didn't pay for it," she tittered, "but it was still an expensive coat." She attacked me with renewed fury.

Like the fight at my apartment, Moira was fast, and her punches felt like steel hammer blows, despite her frail appearance. But now I released the anger and hatred from where I'd contained it after I found out that Sarah was missing. That anger became the fuel that I needed, along with Joe's power, to finally stand up to Moira. I was finally able to withstand her attacks, dodging out of the way or blocking them, when needed. I was also able to land a few of my own attacks and, by the fire burning in Moira's eyes, this surprised her. We were two heavyweight fighters, each trying to land the knockout blow as we danced around the gallery, bloody saltwater swirling around our feet like some horrible tide.

My mother had told me, when I was growing up, that it was wrong to hit a girl. I was sure that she'd approve of me hitting Moira, after what she'd done to Sarah. We continued to trade punches, and we tried to slash each other, but we never connected with anything more than glancing blows that easily healed.

"Stop teasing, Saul," Moira taunted. "Or is this foreplay for you, now?" She licked her lips, in what I assume she thought was a seductive move, but I had seen her true form. She held no attraction for me now.

I feinted a jab with my right hand, causing her to move to the left. "Seems like I hit a nerve," she said. I'd hoped that she would want to rub in salt with her banter, and I followed up the feint with a powerful uppercut that caught her by surprise. It connected under Moira's jaw, which knocked her off her feet and she flew backward. She hit the dying shark, which flailed about in its final gasps of life from Moira's impact, and then she bounced off and landed in the bloody water.

I heard someone yelling behind me. Christian, I think. But I was too focused on Moira to hear what he said.

It took Moira a moment to stand up, and she had to move her jaw back into place with a sickening snap. She narrowed her eyes. "My, my, Saul. Who'd you kill to get so strong?"

"I didn't have to kill anybody," I said, taking a step toward her. "You just finally pissed me off enough when you came after my family."

She shook her head. "I don't believe you. You are no longer the little lamb that I left, barely alive, in your apartment. You have real strength. Real power. Why are you wasting it fighting me? We want the same thing."

I took another step toward Moira, getting within striking distance. I didn't believe a word that Moira said. Too many times, she'd acted all nice and innocent, only to attack me in the next breath.

"I will get Capone," I said. "But I'll do it on my own terms. I don't need you anymore. You may have made me, turned me into the monster that I am, but nobody is my master."

I threw my punch, telegraphing the move, and Moira sneered as she caught my hand in hers. She started to squeeze, and I heard bones snap. I didn't have to fake the grimace of pain that spread across my face, but it did the trick and distracted her. She didn't see my other hand, the claws outstretched. They raked across her neck, catching her by surprise.

She released my hand, and then it was my turn to be surprised. Instead of blood, a black goo oozed out of the wound. It healed just as quickly, but a black stain remained.

"What the hell happened to you?" I asked, taking another step back. Despite my anger at Moira, I felt concern and a bit of pity.

"What happened to me?" Moira gave a bitter laugh. "Why, you did, Saul. *You* happened to me. You killed me."

"What?"

"You jammed a chair leg through my fucking heart, and you killed me." She took a step forward, gesturing to indicate her body. "I'm like this because of you. Did you think I chose to look like a walking corpse? This is all because of you. This is *your fault*."

"Me?"

"Yes, you. If you hadn't been so goddamned stupid, Capone wouldn't have sent me to kill you. You wouldn't have gotten so fucking lucky," she gave a bitter laugh, "and killed me. And Brian wouldn't have had to make the bargain with that she-devil voodoo queen."

"Kalfu?"

Moira nodded, and her eyes took on a red glow, filled with vengeance and hatred. "She used her powers to raise me from the dead, but it didn't turn out like either one of us expected. I'm more than a vampire, more than one of her zombies."

Zombies?

"I'm more powerful than ever, able to do things that Capone would kill to be able to do, but she has power over me. It's just like being under Capone's thumb, all over again."

"Then let's go deal with Kalfu," I said, finally remembering some of what Hoover had wanted us to do. "Maybe together we can stop her and free you."

"And what?" she spat. "I will be like this forever. Killed twice, but never allowed to die. My whole life has been ruined. And for that, I will have my revenge: first on you, and then on Capone."

She started to move forward when there was an explosion from behind me. I felt the bullet fly past me, and I watched as it struck Moira in the chest, and then my vision was obscured by a black mist. I shot a glance over my shoulder to Christian, who was moving the slide on the shotgun to rack another round, and then ran over to Moira. She was tottering on her legs, and I grabbed her in order to keep her from falling.

"Moira," I said, my anger having suddenly evaporated with the gun smoke. I needed Moira to live. "Moira, tell me. Who is Kalfu? Where can I find her? You'll be fine, and then we can stop this."

Moira smiled, and the black 'blood' trickled out. She reached a hand up and I flinched, but she just stroked my cheek. "Saul," she said, her voice weak. "Poor Saul. Your fate was unavoidable." She coughed, some of the black stuff coming out. Her body was trying to heal itself, but it was losing that battle. Already her blouse and coat were soaked, and I could feel the terrible liquid on my hands.

"You need to stop her, Saul. Stop Kalfu."

"Stop her from doing what?"

"What I wanted. She wants more than her kingdom. She wants the night—" She coughed, the noise cutting off her words.

"The night? What about the night?"

Moira looked at me and stroked my cheek again, the anger gone. I stared into her pretty green eyes, seeing tears form in them for the first, and last, time. "You were never—" she coughed again and gave me a wan smile. "Never unremarkable."

Then her eyes glazed over, and I could feel her body crumbling in my hands. As I watched, she turned to dust and ash, her body dissolving into the bloody water. In just a few seconds, I was left holding just her clothes. I looked down, and I could see the leather bracelet that had been on her left wrist floating in the water. I bent down and picked it up, letting her clothes slip from my hands as I pulled it from the water. It was cold to the touch, like I was picking up a block of ice. It burned my skin, so I quickly shoved it into my pocket.

"Huh," Christian said. "That was different."

I turned to Christian, but the anger wouldn't come. Yes, Moira had been a monster. She'd destroyed my life by making me a vampire, and she'd hurt Sarah. I now knew that everything Moira had done had been about revenge: first against Capone, and then against me. She'd only sought the power to get out from under the control of others, and that power had led her down this tragic path. Her desire for revenge had finally consumed her.

"I hope she's finally found peace," I said.

"I hope she's burning in the everlasting fires of Hell," Christian replied.

Chapter 35

Christian and I walked past the dead shark and the other bodies that were laying in several inches of bloody water. "The cops are going to go crazy when they see all of this," I said.

Christian nodded, his mouth set. "That's why we should leave. Now. Someone is bound to show up to work here soon."

I went up to Sarah. She was soaked with the water from the shark tank, but she still looked like she was sleeping, although her eyes were open. I was bending down to pick her up when I saw Christian leveling the shotgun at her. I whirled on him and shoved the barrel of the gun up to the ceiling just as he pulled the trigger. The shot exploded on the ceiling, raining plaster down onto us. "What the hell are you doing? That's my sister," I pointed to her.

"And she's a vampire," Christian said, trying to wrestle the gun back from my grip.

I looked down, seeing the bite mark on her neck. "But she's only been bitten," I said. "That just makes her like you."

I loosened my grip and Christian pulled the gun back. "Take a closer look at her. She's been drained. Completely. That's how a vampire is made. They feed on the victim, and then they kill them. The victim then rises as a vampire. It's what happened to you."

I shook my head. *No. No. This isn't happening.* "My sister is not a vampire."

"She will be if we don't do something about it."

Christian again pointed the weapon at Sarah. I grabbed it again, tearing it from his hands. "We are not going to kill my sister."

"So, you're okay with her becoming like you? Is that what she deserves? To become a monster? An *abomination*?"

I could hear the venom in his words. I stared down at Sarah, tears threatening the corners of my eyes. *I didn't mean for any of this to happen. You were supposed to be safe. I was going to protect you.*

"This is for the best, Saul. Let me end her suffering so that she doesn't become a monster, like you." He held out his hand for the shotgun. The gun shook in my hand.

Oy! Are you really thinking of doing this? Dad's voice rang in my head. *Did I raise a* schmuck? *You made a promise to your mother and me. You promised to bring Sarah home. Safe.*

But not like this.

Like what?

Like me. A monster.

You think that just because some goyim *religious nut thinks that you are a monster that that makes you one? Oy vey! Lord, forgive my stupid son who can't seem to think for himself.*

Saul, Mom said, *You're not a monster. Not to us. And neither is Sarah.*

You will see to that, Dad said. I felt like a kid again, my parents telling me to keep an eye on Sarah at school, to make sure that none of the older students picked on her.

I shifted the shotgun to my left hand. "We are not going

to kill Sarah," I said. Before Christian could argue, I turned to him. "She is not a monster, and neither am I. We didn't ask for any of this, and I will not kill her because of your beliefs. She's not a danger to anybody."

"Are you sure about that?"

"Just as sure as I know that *I'm* not a danger to anybody."

"The jury is still out on that one," Christian said, but he shrugged, and added, "but fine, we'll let your sister... be." He made the sign of the cross as he spoke the last word.

I gave him a long look, waiting for him to finally meet my eyes. When he did, I held his gaze. I didn't use any vampire powers. I just said, "Thank you. Partner."

Christian nodded, and I handed the shotgun back to him. He tucked it under his arm, the barrel pointed at the ground. "What are you going to tell your parents?"

I picked Sarah up. She felt light and vulnerable in my hands. As I settled her over my shoulder, I said, "I don't know. But I'll think of something."

Chapter 36

We left the aquarium before any workers or cops showed up, but somebody would soon find the mess that we'd left behind. There were at least eight dead bodies, plus the clothes of a ninth with no body to go with them. There were also probably twice as many dead fish and sharks, including the massive tiger shark (I'd caught the name on the plaque by the tank) that had to have been the prize of the aquarium. It was going to make the St. Valentine's Day massacre look like a simple mugging, and I couldn't imagine what kind of headlines the afternoon papers would have about it.

The sun was starting to rise over the eastern edge of Lake Michigan, and it looked like it was shaping up to be a nice spring day. Some early risers were already out walking along the shoreline and strolling through Grant Park. We put Sarah into the back seat, and Christian pulled away, the aquarium receding in the side mirrors.

Christian was quiet as he drove, but he kept glancing into the back seat, and then making the sign of the cross. At one point, I'd had enough. "She's not going to leap up and bite you in the neck." At least, I assumed that she wouldn't do that.

"She might," he said. "But that's not why I'm worried."

"What is there to worry about? I'll make sure she's safe and doesn't hurt anybody."

"There's plenty to worry about," he said. "She was made by Moira."

"Who I just killed. She turned to dust in my hands. She's dead for good this time."

"*I* killed her. *You* were playing patty-cake or something with her."

I waved off the jab. I had been confused, my emotions as jumbled and twisted as the ivy at Wrigley Field, but I was glad that Moira was finally dead. "So, Sarah was made by Moira."

"And what was Moira, there at the end?"

"She was a—" I started to say, but stopped, as images came to me. The black blood that oozed from her wounds. The hollow, skeletal appearance of her face. I pulled out the leather bracelet. It was still cold to the touch, but it no longer burned, so I played it through my fingers as if it was a rosary.

"Moira knew that she was different," Christian said "She even said so. And I have never seen a vampire turn to dust like that before. Ever. So, what, in God's name, was she?"

I turned to look at Sarah laying in the back seat. She lay perfectly still, only moving at all from the motion of the car. I had closed her eyes, but that only made her look even more dead than before. I turned back to look out the front of the car. "Do you think Sarah is normal? For a vampire, I mean."

"None of this is normal. I don't think we know what normal is anymore."

I could only acknowledge that as a point of fact. I was certainly not a "normal" vampire anymore, after feeding on Joe to gain some of his power. Moira was certainly not a "normal" vampire at the end. What did that mean for my little sister? I put the bracelet back into my pocket, and we drove a few more blocks in silence.

At a busy intersection, waiting for a trolley to pass, Christian said, "There's still time."

"Time for what?"

"Your parents will grieve, I know, but isn't that better than to bring a mon— a vampire into their lives? A vampire that we don't know anything about? What if she attacks your parents? Could you live with that?"

"I know that she's my sister. That's all that matters."

Christian shrugged, and put the car in gear. In a few minutes, we were driving down the block that I had grown up on. It was then that I realized that this had probably been a bad idea. Despite the early hour, it seemed like everybody in the neighborhood was outside to enjoy this fine spring day. Families sat on the steps to their buildings, talking and laughing. Windows were already open to air out the apartments. Despite it being a Saturday, *Shabbat*, and a day for prayer and attending Temple, many of the men were heading to their jobs, since the *goyim* only recognized Sunday as a day of rest.

"As soon as we get out of the car, everybody in the neighborhood will know that we brought Sarah home, sick or injured," I said. "Or worse."

"Should we go someplace else?"

"No," I said. "Sarah deserves to find out who she is now at home. My parents deserve to know that she's alive."

Christian raised an eyebrow.

"You know what I mean."

He nodded, and drove slowly up the street, pulling up outside my parent's building and double parking next to the other cars along the curb.

I got out of the car, trying to ignore the exclamations

from people that I'd lived next to for practically my entire life, who had all heard that I had died. Hell, most of them had probably attended my funeral and said prayers over my coffin with my parents, consoling them about my loss, telling them platitudes that things would be better, that I was in a better place. Now they were seeing me, apparently back from the dead, pulling my sister, who looked more dead than alive right now, from the back of the car. I could hear the quiet exclamations, the words of shock and amazement coming from the crowd.

Christian walked ahead of me, so that he could open the door to the building. I smiled politely to friends and neighbors, people I hadn't seen in over a year, as I carried Sarah up the steps. "The gossip mill will be busy tonight," I said, as I went inside.

"Tonight? I think within the next ten seconds," Christian said, as he smiled and tipped his hat to the assembled crowd.

We went up to my parent's apartment, and I knocked. I could hear Dad calling out and heading to the door, but it was Mrs. Gershowitz's door that opened first. I heard a gasp come from her as she took in the sight. Finally, Dad opened the door.

"Saul! *Oy vey,* and Sarah. My god, what happened?" He looked past me to see Mrs. Gershowitz standing in her doorway. "Come in, come in," he said, ushering us into the apartment. "Go back inside, Greta," Dad told Mrs. Gershowitz. "I'm sure Miriam will fill you in over coffee later today."

Dad closed the door, but I didn't stop in the entryway. Dad started asking questions, while Mom came out of the kitchen. She started weeping when she saw Sarah, and tried to grab her from my arms. I headed to Sarah's bedroom, and I laid her, as gently as I could, on her bed. She was still wet from the flooding at the aquarium, and she smelled like the ocean at low tide, but I didn't care. I certainly wasn't going to change her into clean, dry clothes. Not my sister.

Mom burst in after me. "Oh, Saul! You found her. My baby is safe."

She sat down on the bed, before I could stop her, and took Sarah's hand in hers. She pushed strands of wet hair off of Sarah's forehead. She turned to me. "What's wrong with her?"

"She'll be fine, Mom," I said.

"Why does she smell like the fish market? Did you find her there? Is that where the kidnappers had her?" Dad stood in the doorway, clearly making up his mind about what had happened.

I put my hands on Mom's shoulders and gently lifted her off the bed. "She's going to be fine," I assured her. "In a couple of days. She just needs to rest now."

I led her away from the bed, and I ushered her and Dad both out of the bedroom and into the living room. Christian still stood by the door, smiling politely, with a smug expression that only I could see. He was enjoying himself as he watched me fumble with my parents. I steered Mom to the couch, while Dad sat down in his armchair. I walked over to the bookcase and took down a copy of *The Great Gatsby* from the shelf and pulled out the flask that Dad kept hidden inside.

"Saul Abraham Imbierowicz!" Mom exclaimed. "It's barely after breakfast." I winced at her use of my full name, but I ignored it, opened the flask, and took a drink. The harsh liquor burned the back of my throat, but it managed to calm my nerves. I handed the flask to Dad.

He responded to Mom's glare of disapproval with a

shrug, and then he tilted the flask to his lips. He then waved his hand at me. "Well, are you going to tell us what happened, or do your mother and I have to wait until our old age to find out?"

I held out my hand for the flask, but Dad snatched the book away and nestled the flask back within the pages.

What do I say? I asked myself. *What do I tell them?* I looked at Mom and Dad, expecting some insight to come from their voices in my head, but they were unusually quiet this morning.

That's because they're just in your head. The real ones are sitting right in front of you, Sarah's voice said. *And you better come up with a good lie,* nudnik. *It looks like they're getting antsy.*

I should lie to them?

Do you think they'll understand anything if you tell them the truth? Don't be a shmendrik. *Vampires. Voodoo. Sharks! I don't believe half of it, and I was there.*

You weren't there.

Yes, I was, Sarah huffed.

Being unconscious on the floor doesn't count.

She couldn't admit that I was right, and said, *You can't tell Mom and Dad the truth. Dad will ask a million questions and still not believe you, and you'll probably give Mom a stroke.*

I looked up to Christian, who stood behind Dad's armchair. He still had that smug look on his face. I gave him my best *what do I do?* look, but he just shrugged and made the sign of the cross. *A lot of help he is. Some partner.*

"The kidnappers, they took her to a fish market down near Indiana," I said, picking up on Dad's comment from earlier. Keep it simple. Keep it something that he already believes. "They drugged Sarah to keep her quiet."

"Drugged?" Mom put a hand to her mouth. "Why?"

Shit. Why did they take you?

I don't know. Sarah said. *Maybe I was some guy's moll, and they kidnapped me to get to him!*

No! Do you want Mom and Dad to think that you're sneaking out of the house to be a gangster's girl? They'll never let you out of their sight again.

"I don't think we will ever know the exact reason," I said, stalling for time. "But these kidnappers were also running whiskey out of Canada, so Ness had been keeping an eye on them for some time. They must have gotten wind that I was on the team, and they thought that they could use Sarah as leverage against us. They drugged her to keep her quiet, so the neighbors wouldn't know that she was there."

Not bad, said Sarah. *But I think it would've been better if I'd been a moll.*

I had to agree with Sarah that I'd spun a pretty good lie for Mom and Dad. Heck, even Christian seemed impressed. She was wrong about being a moll, though. Dad would have killed her himself.

"If Sarah was drugged, then we need to call a doctor." Dad started to get up from the armchair. "I'll give Dr. Greenberg a call."

"No," I said. "We don't need a doctor. The drugs will wear off in a day or two, and she'll be back to normal when that happens." I saw Christian roll his eyes, and did my best to ignore him.

"And these kidnappers," Dad said. "You stopped them?"

"Yes. Nobody is going to hurt Sarah again."

Chapter 37

I walked into the diner on the ground floor of the Post Office. I hadn't been here in over a year, but I felt a bit of nostalgia as I took a seat in one of the booths. I had only worked in the Post Office for a few weeks before Moira and Capone had changed everything. I didn't miss my job—and I guess I had to give credit to Moira and Capone for pulling me away from that monotony—but I missed the times that Joe and I had spent here on our breaks or after work.

The waitress came over, an older woman with mousy brown hair. Her nametag read, "Gladys". "What'll ya have, hun?"

"Where's Francine?" I asked. After everything that had happened in the past week, I think I was looking for some connection to my past.

"Who?"

"Francine. She's a waitress who works here. About your height, long brown hair, freckles. At least, she used to work here."

The waitress paused, and then said, "Yeah, I think I remember her. She left around the same time that I started, about six months ago."

"Where'd she go?" I didn't know why I asked, but I guess I was disappointed. Yet another part of my past had gone.

"She moved out of town. Down to Missouri. Kansas City, or St. Louis, maybe."

"Oh. Too bad." I gave her a smile. "Can I get a cup of Joe and a slice of pie?"

"Sure thing, hun." She walked off, and I had to ponder just how much my life had changed since last year.

The waitress came back with my coffee and a slice of apple pie. Just then, the door opened and Christian walked in.

"Hey, partner," I said, around a mouthful of pie.

Christian sat down, tossing his hat and a newspaper onto the table. "That looks good." He motioned for Gladys. "Can I get the same, please?"

In a moment, she'd delivered his pie and coffee. I glanced at the headline that ran across the entire front page, practically screaming the news: AQUARIUM MASSA-CRE.

"Can you believe that Capone has already offered to donate to the repairs to the aquarium?" I asked.

"Right after he denied having any part in that 'horrible, tragic event'," Christian said, with a snort.

"And the press just ate it up," I said, "like they always do."

"You could be that persuasive if you wanted," Christian offered.

I shoved the paper aside. "Hey, I only use my powers for good."

Christian grunted, and rolled his eyes. "They're saying that the aquarium will still open at the end of May."

"Maybe we can go back and see the shark exhibit when it does."

"No, thank you," Christian said, as he drank his coffee. "I've seen enough sharks for a lifetime."

I smiled, and drank my own coffee. I wasn't too keen on seeing the sharks any time soon, either.

"How's Sarah doing?"

I set my cup down with a sigh. "No change. She still hasn't come out of her coma or whatever it is."

"It's called being dead. She's dead, Saul."

I shrugged. "Potato. Poh-tah-to. She's supposed to wake up, and she hasn't done that yet."

"I told you that it will take a couple of days. That's what happens when a vampire is created." Christian had lowered his voice.

"I know. I was just hoping…"

Christian shook his head. "The only relief she can have now—"

"No," I said, cutting him off.

Christian frowned. "I was going to say that her only relief now is for you to be there for her. She's going to be confused. You need to be her support."

I hung my head, feeling my cheeks flush. "I will. I spent all night there last night, and all day today."

"How are your parents taking it?"

"Okay. But I had to keep telling them not to call for a doctor and not to let any neighbors in."

"You didn't…"

I opened my mouth in shock. "No. I'd never use my power on Mom and Dad. It would have made things a lot easier, though."

"Do they still buy the kidnapping story?"

"Yeah," I finished my coffee and pulled out my Chesterfields. "Dad keeps asking for details, but I think he's just curious. He listens to too many cop dramas on the radio, and he wants to be part of the action."

I lit my cigarette. "Mom is just happy to have Sarah

home. She's not curious about what happened at all."

"And what about you?" Christian asked, finishing his own coffee.

"Me?"

"Your parents thought you were dead for over a year. Don't they want to know what you've been doing?"

"Dad does. He likes that I work for Ness. He's asked me a couple of times what it's like. I don't tell him much."

"Well, look on the bright side. You don't work for Ness any longer."

"Yeah, and telling him that I work for J. Edgar Hoover would be an improvement?"

"What about your mom?"

"Mom is still mad at me. She's glad that I brought Sarah home, but she thinks that I was pretending to be dead just to spite her for... I don't know what."

Christian gave a small laugh, and then checked his watch. "Come on, we've got a few minutes before we have to meet Ness."

I nodded and finished my cigarette. I left a dollar on the table, and we headed out of the diner.

Chapter 38

We left the diner and walked further into the building. As we passed the information desk, I remembered the night that I had sneaked around it to find out where the two Feds—Christian and Truesdale—were working. I wondered if the veteran who worked the desk back then still did.

"Why did Ness want to meet us here?" I asked.

"I don't know," Christian said, as he pushed the elevator call button. "He just said to meet him here, on the sixth floor, at nine o'clock."

"I thought we didn't work for Ness anymore," I said, as we got into the elevator.

"We don't, but it's best to not burn any bridges." He pushed the button for the sixth floor. "Besides, he asked politely."

"What about Hoover?"

"What about him?"

"Well, we work for him now, right? When do we meet with him to tell him what we learned from Moira?"

"What exactly *did* we learn from that witch?" Christian asked.

"Not much," I admitted. "But still, aren't we supposed to report in, tell somebody about it?"

"Welcome to the Night Watchers, Saul. We get a lot of orders, but almost no supervision." The elevator stopped, and the doors opened. "It's a blessing and a curse," Christian finished.

Eliot Ness stood in the hallway, folding up a newspaper as we got off the elevator. He looked tired, like he hadn't slept. He tapped the headline on the paper. "I'm assuming this was the two of you." He was smiling as he said it, but I still felt like he'd accused me of doing something wrong.

"To be fair, it was Capone's men that did most of the damage," I said.

"Yeah, Saul here only destroyed one of the tanks," Christian added, with a laugh.

Ness gave a chuckle. "Well, I'm glad that I don't have to deal with your mess, for once."

"Why are we here?" I asked, trying to sound nonchalant.

"You're going to need to learn how to be tactful if you're going to work for Mr. Hoover," Ness said. It was said in a tone of friendly advice, but I still felt my cheeks redden.

"Mr. Hoover asked me to show the two of you to your new office," Ness continued. He turned to the right, and headed down the hall.

I looked at Christian. "Not the janitor's closet again."

He just shrugged and followed Ness. I headed after them. Ness turned the corner, and I saw the door to the janitor's closet straight ahead. But Ness stopped in front of the other door, the one that had belonged to the postal inspector, although I saw that his name had been scraped off of the frosted glass of the door. The lights were on inside, and I could smell cigar smoke and aftershave.

Ness pushed open the door, and we walked into the office. J. Edgar Hoover stood in the center of the office. He wore the same dark suit from the other night, holding a cigar in one hand and the paper in the other. The office was bigger than the janitor's closet, but it didn't seem much bigger. It was also currently empty. No desks, no chairs, not even a wastebasket.

"Welcome to your new home," Hoover said.

"I love what you've done with the place." I couldn't keep the sarcasm out of my voice.

"You can requisition desks and chairs and anything else you need," Ness said.

Hoover narrowed his eyes as he held up the paper, the headline leaping off the front page. "What the hell did you two do?"

I wanted to tell Hoover where he could shove his attitude, but Christian spoke first.

"The situation got out of hand, sir."

"Out of hand?" Hoover snorted. "That's the fucking understatement of the year, Agent Wright." He tossed the paper at Christian with a contemptuous flick of his hand. "Do I have to remind you that the Night Watchers are a *secret* organization? We work from the shadows. We are a rumor, recognizable only as déjà vu and dismissed just as quickly. We don't exist; anonymity is our name. Silence our native tongue."

I rolled my eyes, but Ness and Christian seemed to be lapping this up.

"But that's impossible to do when you go and fucking destroy major tourist attractions," Hoover finished.

"It's not like we had a choice in the matter," I said.

Hoover glared at me. "You always have a choice, Agent Imbierowicz. Our job works a lot easier when we are not shooting up the place like the fucking Wild West. You work for me now, and I have a higher standard that I expect you to meet."

I think I saw Ness actually bite his tongue at that.

"We understand, sir," Christian said. "It won't happen again."

I kept my mouth shut, and Hoover gave me a curt nod that said that keeping silent was the most intelligent thing I had ever done in my life. That almost made me say something, but instead, I just smiled. That earned me a rare, and very quick, smile from Hoover.

"So, what did you two manage to learn while you were doling out major property damage?" Hoover asked. "Where is Kalfu hiding?"

"We don't know," I said.

Hoover barked a laugh, but it was bitter and lacked any mirth. I guess my moment of approval from Hoover was over. "All that damage, and we got zilch for it."

"It was a dynamic situation," Christian tried to explain, but Hoover shut him up with a glare. He turned his gaze back to me.

I was tired of Hoover's holier-than-thou attitude. I straightened up, took a step closer to Hoover, and I let just a bit of who I really was come out. It was nothing like what I'd done back in Ness's office, but more like the look that I'd given Capone's goon at the Lexington Hotel. Hoover managed to keep his face impassive, but I saw his pupils widen just a bit.

"Moira died in my arms, and she turned to ash. She died once before, over a year ago, when I shoved a chair leg through her heart, but Kalfu brought her back from the dead. Moira was paying off that debt to Kalfu. She apparently needed Moira to protect her from another vampire."

"Another vampire?" Hoover asked. "Geez, you're like cockroaches."

I did my best to ignore the comment. "Kalfu told Moira that she was promised a kingdom."

"A kingdom? From whom? Where?"

"Beats me," I said. "Moira didn't give me any details. I think this other vampire may want the same thing, or wants to keep Kalfu from getting it."

Hoover listened to everything, and then took a pull on his cigar. I started to say something else, but he held up a finger. After a moment, he started nodding his head.

"It's amazing that you managed to do it, but you probably did something helpful in all of this mess."

I glanced at Christian, who just shrugged, and asked, "Why did Kalfu want Moira as protection from another vampire?"

"I don't know," I said.

"It doesn't matter," Hoover said. "With Moira dead for good, that means that part of Kalfu's plan is ruined. That gives us time to figure out what she's doing in Chicago."

"Let's go ask Capone," Christian said. "He's always bragging that nothing goes on in the city that he doesn't know about."

"That will be easy to do with Capone behind bars," Ness said. He stood in the corner of the office, trying to stay out of our conversation with Hoover.

"You arrested Capone?" I asked. I was surprised that such a big story hadn't made it into the papers.

"Not yet," Ness said. "I'm going to do it tomorrow."

"For tax evasion?" Christian asked.

"It should be for murder," I said.

"We don't always get what we want," Ness said. "But this tax charge will stick."

"Good," said Hoover. "He's been enough of a pain in the ass. It's not sexy, but it will get him off the street. It will show the American people that the rule of law matters."

"Well, that's good. They need something, since apparently everybody in the country is ignoring the Volstead Act," I said. Hoover actually chuckled.

"I'd rather put a stake through his heart," said Christian. "He's a monster."

"He'll be off the street and no longer causing trouble," Hoover said. "That's good enough for me."

"I want to be there," I said. "Let me and Christian arrest him."

Ness started to shake his head, but Hoover said, "I think that's a good idea. It seems fitting somehow that Saul finishes this. Closing the book on this particular chapter in our history. Besides," he nodded to me, "if Capone is stupid enough to put up a fight, Saul is the best one of us to stand up to him. Always bring your big guns to ensure that the other side doesn't try something with theirs."

Ness let out a breath. Clearly, he was regretting that he'd even brought up the subject, but I could see on his face that he was resigned to Hoover's suggestion. "Fine, you can both come along. Meet us at the office tomorrow morning at ten."

Chapter 39

It was just before noon when the cars pulled up outside the Lexington Hotel. It had rained earlier in the morning, but now the clouds were parting, and the sun was breaking through: an auspicious sign. The doors on the cars all opened simultaneously, and we all got out. Barney Cloonan, Ness, Christian, and I got out of the lead car, while Tom Friel, Lyle Chapman, Bill Gardner, and Mike King got out of the second. The rest of Ness's team were waiting down at the main police station where we would take Capone after his arrest.

Ness had wanted a show of force, not only to show the people of Chicago, and the nation, that nobody was above the law, but also to impress upon Capone that it would be pointless to resist.

As we walked up to the hotel, there were flashes from a couple of newspapermen. I wasn't sure if they just hung out here in case anything newsworthy ever happened, or if Ness had tipped them off. It would certainly be good press for Ness, and it was something that he had done before.

The doorman opened the doors, and we strode across the lobby of the Lexington. Dozens of heads turned to watch us. None of us openly carried any weapons, but Ness was recognizable from the papers. It was clear to anybody who saw us what we were here to do.

The usual stooges stood by the elevators and tried to

block our way. They didn't pull their guns, but their posture said that they wouldn't hesitate to do so.

Before Ness could pull his badge or say anything, I said, "Step aside." The command had them moving away from the elevators before they knew what they were doing.

Ness whispered to me, "I am going to miss that."

I smiled as Christian opened the elevator. He, Ness, Cloonan, and I got in. Ness told the other four to keep the area clear, and that we'd be back down soon. We rode up in silence, and stepped out onto Capone's floor. Frank Nitti stood in the hallway, a look of surprise on his face.

"We're here to see your boss," Christian said, shoving Nitti out of the way. Ness didn't wait, and headed down the hallway to Capone's suite. We all followed, Nitti protesting as he brought up the rear.

Ness didn't bother to knock, and he opened the door to the waiting area. I stepped up and opened the door to Capone's office. Al Capone sat at a round table that had been laid out for lunch. His suit coat was off, and the sleeves of his green silk shirt were rolled up to his elbows. He was setting down a glass of red liquid as we walked in. It might have looked like wine to the others, but I could smell the scent of blood.

"Surprised to see us, Al?" I asked. I couldn't help but taunt him.

Capone calmly picked up a napkin and dabbed at his lips. "Mr. Imbierowicz," Capone said. Behind me I heard Cloonan say, "Who?"

"Nothing surprises me," Capone said. "Whatever it is you are here for is insignificant. I am untouchable." He spread his hands and gave a broad smile.

I smiled back as Ness said, "Not this time, Mr. Capone." He pulled out a folded piece of paper from his coat. "This is a federal warrant for your arrest for failure to pay income taxes."

Christian and I stepped up to the table. Christian pulled out a pair of handcuffs. I stared at Capone, my expression daring him to try something.

"This is a bunch of bullshit," Capone said. "I'll beat your rap, like I beat all the others." He threw his napkin down onto the table. "You can't make any of this stick. Everybody in this town knows who I am. Everybody knows not to mess with me. I *am* Chicago."

Christian grabbed Capone's elbow and lifted him out of his seat. I was surprised, and a bit disappointed that Capone didn't try to resist.

"I'll beat this rap," Capone repeated. "Nobody treats me like this. *Nobody.*"

Through all of this, Ness just stood there and smiled, tapping the warrant against his palm. "Yes, everybody in Chicago knows you. Some even fear you. But not me, and not the federal government."

I grabbed Capone's hands and brought them together with almost no resistance, as Christian put the handcuffs on. I leaned close to Capone and whispered, "There are two things in life that are unavoidable: death and taxes. You may have cheated death, but you can't cheat on your taxes."

Epilogue

"How's she doing?" Dad stood in the doorway to Sarah's room. I sat in a chair, watching my sister. Sarah lay on her bed in the same place that I'd laid her Saturday morning. She hadn't been breathing then, and still wasn't now, and that was a fact I had kept from Mom and Dad.

"Still sleeping," I lied. "But no other change."

"Let me call Dr. Greenberg, son. Maybe he can do something. Your mom, she's getting worried."

"Dad, there's nothing Dr. Greenberg, or any other doctor, can do for Sarah." *Man, was that an understatement.* I turned to look at Dad. "We just need to give her time to let the drugs get out of her system."

Dad stepped up behind me. "She looks so peaceful sleeping there, but why won't she wake up?"

When Christian had asked me yesterday if I had used my powers on my parents, I hadn't been fully truthful with him. I hadn't used my powers to command them not to call a doctor, but Sarah lying dead in her bed would have been a problem. I suggested to them that Sarah was just sleeping, and they believed me, even though they never saw her take a breath.

"She will," I said. "In fact, she's been getting better." I stood up and put my arm on Dad's shoulders. "I think that she'll be awake by the morning."

At least, I hope she will. I had no experience to go on,

except for my own, and I hadn't been awake—alive—for that. Eliot Ness had told me that I had been dead for two days before I woke up in my new apartment. It had been two days for Sarah, so I expected—hoped—that she'd come back tonight.

"Go to bed, Dad." I started to lead him out of the room, but he slipped out of my embrace and walked over to the bed.

"Good night, lambchop," he whispered, using my sister's nickname. She'd loved it when she was younger, but had tried to get him to stop using it in the past couple of years. He leaned over and kissed her forehead.

He turned to me, pointing his finger. "You wake me. If anything changes, you wake me up."

"I will, Dad," I lied again.

Dad nodded and walked out, while I sat back down in the chair. He paused to look back at Sarah and me. "You did good, Saul," he said, and then he left and closed the door.

"No, I didn't," I whispered. I looked at Sarah, new guilt piling up onto the old like worn clothes waiting for laundry day.

I had failed my parents and Sarah. I hadn't been able to keep her safe. I hadn't been able to prevent Moira from doing this to her. *I shouldn't have taken the time to go see Joe. That had been my mistake.*

Sure, nudnik, Sarah's voice said, and I had to take a look to make sure that it was only in my head. *Moira would have mopped the floor with you without Joe's help. You'd be dead—for real—and I'd still be like this.*

I could have done more, I told myself. *I didn't try hard enough. I was too slow.*

"It was all my fault," I said, to the room.

"You got that right, big brother."

At first, I thought that I'd imagined the voice in my head, but then I looked and saw Sarah, her eyes open and looking at me. "Sarah?"

"I don't know what it was," she said, her voice scratchy, "but I'm sure it was your fault."

She tried to sit up, and I moved to help her. As I sat down again, she looked at me, her eyes going wide. "Wait a sec. You're dead. We had a funeral for you." She reached out a hand to pinch me, to make sure that I was real. "Does Mom know you're alive? She's going to be so mad at you."

I couldn't help but smile. "She knows," I said, "And she is." I reached down and picked up my Thermos. "But I *am* dead. And so are you."

She stared at me for a second, and then started to laugh, but stopped herself, her eyes staring past me, to something in the far distance. I unscrewed the cap and poured the contents into the metal cup.

"I remember a woman with red hair and pasty skin," she said. "She took me from here to someplace that smelled like fish."

I nodded. "Her name was—"

"Moira," Sarah finished. She turned to glare at me. "And she said that she took me because of you. Then she... she bit me," her eyes went wide, and her hand went up to her neck, touching the spot where Moira had bitten her. The wound had healed within the first day.

"This *was* your fault," she said. Her accusation piled on more guilt. "She was so mad at you, she wanted to kill you. But she wanted you to know that she'd gotten to me, first."

"I'm sorry, Sarah. I tried to stop her. I tried to keep her from hurting you."

"You didn't try hard enough. She bit me. She—"

221

Sarah's eyes went even wider than before. She turned to me, her mouth agape. "She killed me," she whispered, her lower lip quivering.

"I know. I'm sorry."

"I'm dead." She paused, and looked around the room. "Wait. If I'm dead, then how can I be here?"

She turned to me again, "What did you do to me, Saul?"

"I didn't do anything. It was Moira. She killed you."

"Then how can I be alive now?"

"Here, drink this," I said, handing the cup of blood to Sarah. I knew that she was probably feeling like she'd never eaten in her entire life. "Drink this, slowly."

Sarah hesitated, but then put the cup to her lips. I could tell when she tasted the blood, as her eyes went wide, and she looked like she was about to spit it out. But then something clicked, and she swallowed, draining the entire cup.

"You did better than me the first time," I said. I took the cup back from her to fill it again.

"You?" she turned to look at me. "What?"

"Sarah," I started to say, but then paused. I hadn't really practiced how I was going to tell her what had happened. What we had both become. "I was killed last year, at the end of February. I was shot. By Al Capone."

Sarah's eyes widened, "*The* Al Capone?"

I nodded. "On the Michigan Avenue bridge. It was snowing, and he shot me several times."

"Why?"

"It doesn't really matter now," I said. "But then, like you, I woke up in a new apartment. No longer dead." I held the cup in my hands and stared at it.

"You and me, Sarah. We're vampires."

"Vampires? Like in that book, *Dracula*?" She was starting to shake, and I set the cup down and took her hands.

"Sarah, look at me." She turned to look, her eyes wide with fear.

"Yes, we are vampires, but not like Dracula. It's complicated. But I will explain everything. I will be by your side."

"Vampires," she said, her expression softening. "Boy, Mom and Dad are going to be pissed when they find out."

I chuckled, and handed the cup of blood to Sarah. "Which is why they can never find out."

She drank slower this time, but still drained it in one gulp. She held the cup in her lap. "So, whose blood am I drinking?"

"It's cow's blood," I said.

"You mean, we don't drink blood from people?"

"Some do, but I don't," I lied. *Yeah, I lied. I said it was complicated. Why make it scarier than it needed to be for her?*

"You're lying," she said, but then shook her head. "But it's okay. I'd probably lie, too, if I had to kill people to eat."

"It's going to be okay, Sarah." I put my hand on hers, giving it a gentle squeeze. "When I went through this, I had nobody. I had to learn everything on my own. But you've got me."

She rolled her eyes, "*Gevalt.* God help me, then," but she smiled as she said it.

She handed the cup back to me, and gave me a hug. "Thank you, big brother."

I didn't say anything, just returned the hug. After a moment, she pulled back and looked me in the eyes.

"So, what do we do now?"

Author's Notes

Thank you for reading our books. We hope you have found them as entertaining to read as we have writing them. In three novels, we have explored an alternate history where vampires and other supernatural creatures exist. We've explored a world where one of America's biggest gangsters, Al Capone, was actually a vampire. To tell our story across this trilogy, we've taken a few dramatic liberties with Al Capone's life—in addition to making him one of the living dead. For *Unavoidable*, we've sped up many of the events surrounding Capone's eventual arrest and charges for tax evasion, and kept Eliot Ness involved for the sake of our story. Al Capone was arrested in Philadelphia in May 1929 for carrying a concealed weapon. He was sentenced to a year in prison, and served only ten months before he was released. (Al Capone *was* released a day early from Eastern State Penitentiary. The prison warden had removed Capone to another prison a day before his official release day, supposedly for Capone's "safety" and to spare him harassment from the press.)

While we've altered the events to suit our story, the real event around Al Capone and the charges of tax evasion that finally put Capone in prison for good are just as interesting. The actual tax case for Capone started on April 17, 1930, when he was questioned about his income by IRS agent Frank Wilson. Wilson and federal prosecutor George E. Q.

Johnson then built their case against Capone for tax evasion. On June 16, 1931, Al Capone pled guilty to tax evasion and prohibition charges. It was a plea bargain arrangement between Johnson, the US Attorney General, and Capone's lawyers. Everything seemed to be arranged, but Capone was not taken to prison right away, and he boasted to the press that he had struck a deal for a two-and-a-half-year sentence. The presiding judge for the case, Judge James Wilkerson, had apparently been angered by press reports that he was just signing off on the agreement, and so, on July 30, 1931, the day of sentencing, he told both sets of lawyers that only a judge could hand down a sentence, and he wouldn't do it without hearing evidence. Both sides were shocked, and Capone immediately changed his plea to not guilty.

Capone's trial started on October 3, 1931, and it started badly for Capone. The IRS agent, Frank Wilson, had gotten wind that Capone and his men were trying to rig the jury selection, passing out $1,000 bills, promising political jobs, and even making threats. Wilson told Judge Wilkerson and, at the last minute, he switched the jury pool with another judge. The trial commenced, and on October 17, 1931, the jury found Al Capone guilty of three felony counts and two misdemeanor counts out of the twenty-two total charges that had been brought against him. A week later, Judge Wilkerson sentenced Al Capone to eleven years in federal prison, fined him $50,000, and charged him $7,692 for court costs, in addition to the $215,000 plus interest that was due on back taxes. Al Capone had finally met his match. He appealed, but his appeals were denied, and he then served his time in the US Penitentiary in Atlanta, Georgia, and then at Alcatraz.

Certainly, this is not the way Hollywood (or writers)

like to portray Capone, and how he was finally defeated. It does lack a certain amount of dramatic appeal, but it is still fascinating. We recommend several books on Capone's life if you want to learn more about who he really was: *Get Capone: The Secret Plot that Captured America's Most Wanted Gangster* by Jonathan Eig, *Mr. Capone: The Real—and Complete—Story of Al Capone* by Robert J. Schoenberg, and *Capone: The Life and World of Al Capone* by John Kobler.

The Shedd Aquarium opened to the public in May of 1930. John G. Shedd wanted an attraction that would set a standard for years to come, and that would outdo every other aquarium in the world. At the time, it was described as a "neoclassical temple of white marble and terra cotta that celebrates aquatic life, from the marine fossils in its limestone floor to Neptune's trident capping its glass dome." It was the first inland aquarium with permanent saltwater exhibits, and they used 20 insulated railroad tank cars that traveled between Chicago and Key West, Florida, to deliver a million gallons of tropical ocean water for the exhibits. As far as we know, there were never any shootouts at the aquarium, and there were no delays in opening to the public. We don't know if there were any sharks in the exhibits when it opened, and it's doubtful that they had a tiger shark, so we hope we can be forgiven for a bit of artistic license to make for a fun climax to our story.

There is not a pool hall in Chicago by the name of Pandora's Legacy (that we know of). It *is* the name of a wonderful science fiction book written by a great friend of ours, Eric Michael Craig, who was gracious enough to allow us to kill him in our story. He's a fantastic writer, and we highly recommend his books.

A big thank you to our beta readers! Without you, this

story would not be what it is. You have helped us find plot holes, continuity errors, and apparently every grammar sin ever committed, so we are grateful to your support and your efforts to make this a better book.

About the Authors

The writing duo of Geoff Habiger and Coy Kissee have been life-long friends since high school in Manhattan, Kansas. (Affectionately known as the Little Apple, which was a much better place to grow up than the Big Apple, in our humble opinion.) We love reading, baseball, cats, role-playing games, comics, and board games (not necessarily in that order and sometimes the cats can be very trying). We've spent many hours together over the years (and it's been many years) basically geeking out and talking about our favorite books, authors, and movies, often discussing what we would do differently to fix a story or make a better script. We eventually turned this passion into something more than just talk and now write the stories that we want to read.

Coy lives with his wife in Lenexa, Kansas. Geoff lives with his wife and son in Tijeras, New Mexico.